HERE BE MONSTERS!
KT-195-794
15 286 721 7

Also by Alan Snow

Worse Things Happen at Sea

HERE BE MONSTERS!
by Alan Snow

OXFORD
UNIVERSITY PRESS

OXFORD
UNIVERSITY PRESS

Great Clarendon Street, Oxford OX2 6DP
Oxford University Press is a department of the University of Oxford.
It furthers the University's objective of excellence in research, scholarship,
and education by publishing worldwide in

Oxford New York

Auckland Cape Town Dar es Salaam Hong Kong Karachi
Kuala Lumpur Madrid Melbourne Mexico City Nairobi
New Delhi Shanghai Taipei Toronto

With offices in

Argentina Austria Brazil Chile Czech Republic France Greece
Guatemala Hungary Italy Japan Poland Portugal Singapore
South Korea Switzerland Thailand Turkey Ukraine Vietnam

Oxford is a registered trade mark of Oxford University Press
in the UK and in certain other countries

First published 2005
First published in this edition 2014

British Library Cataloguing in Publication Data
Data available

ISBN: 978-0-19-273930-8

1 3 5 7 9 10 8 6 4 2

Printed in Great Britain
Paper used in the production of this book is a natural,
recyclable product made from wood grown in sustainable forests
The manufacturing process conforms to the environmental
regulations of the country of origin

To Edward, and with enormous thanks to everyone who has helped along the way

Here Be Monsters

Contents

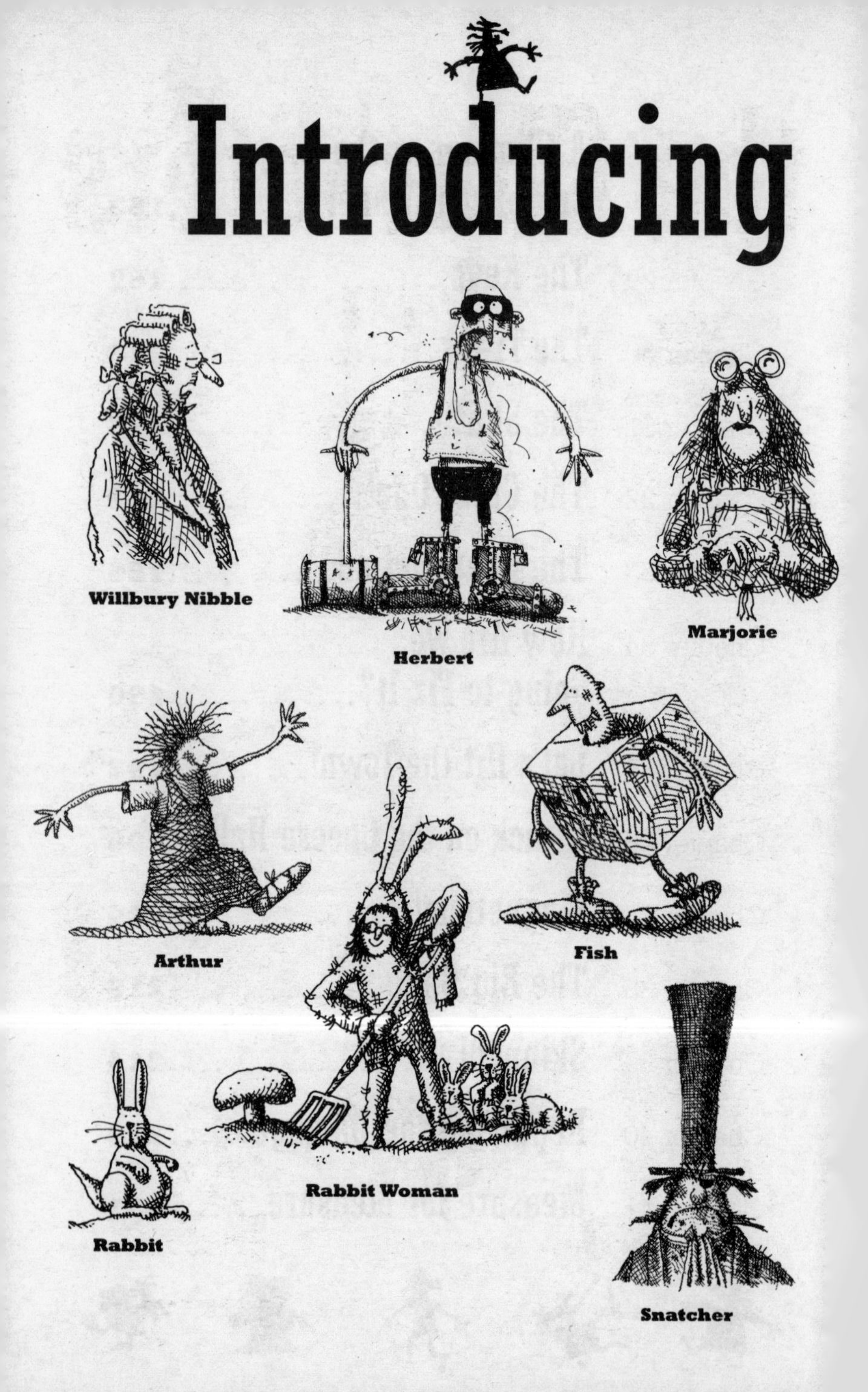
Introducing
Willbury Nibble
Herbert
Marjorie
Arthur
Fish
Rabbit Woman
Rabbit
Snatcher

the Characters

Captain

The Members

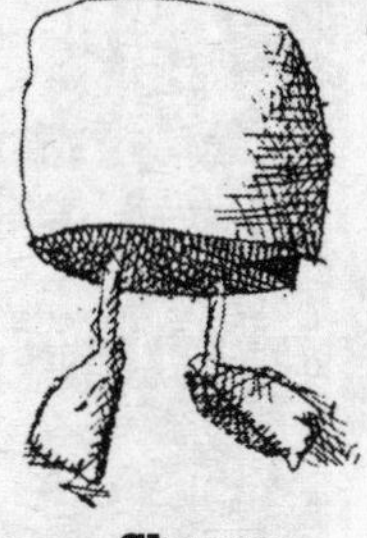

Cheese

Grandfather

Framley

Trotting Badger

Crow

Cabbagehead

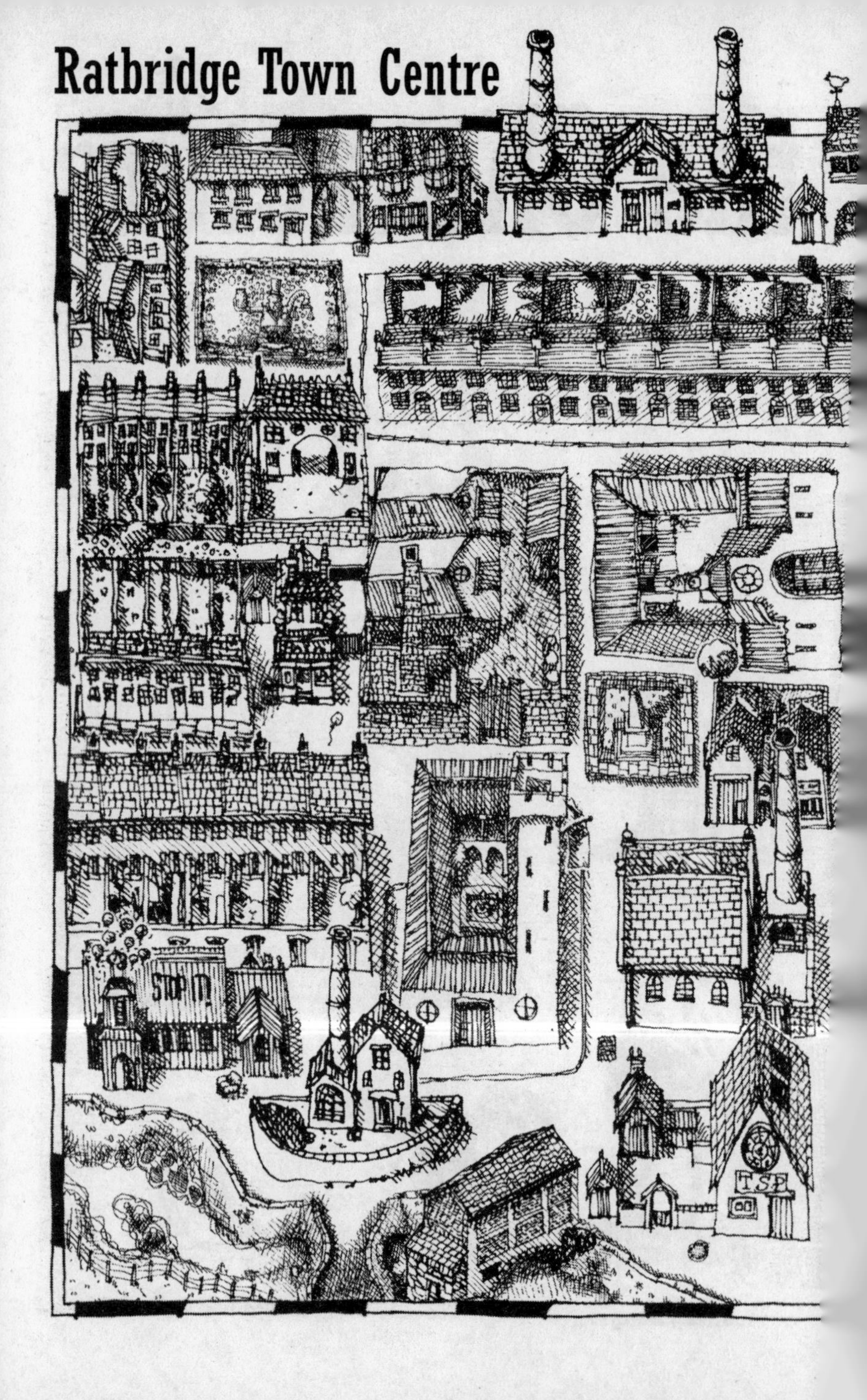
Ratbridge Town Centre
STOP IT!
TSP

Chapter 1

Coming Up!

It was a late Sunday evening and Ratbridge stood silver grey and silent in the moonlight. Early evening rain had washed away the cloud of smoke that normally hung over the town, and now long shadows from the factory chimneys fell across oily puddles in the empty streets. The town was at rest.

In the lane that ran behind Fore Street a heavy iron drain cover set amongst the cobbles moved. Something was pushing it up from below.

One side of the cover lifted a few inches, and from beneath it, a pair of eyes scanned the lane. The drain cover lifted further, then slid sideways. A boy's head wearing a woven helmet with nine or ten antennae rose

through the hole and glanced around. The boy shut his eyes, and he listened. For a moment all was quiet, then a distant dog bark echoed off the walls. Silence returned. The boy opened his eyes, reached out of the hole, and pulled himself up and out into the lane. He was dressed very strangely, in a large vest knitted from soft rope, which reached the ground, and under that a short one-piece suit made from old sugar sacks. His feet were wrapped in layers of rough cloth, tied with string.

Fixed about his body by wide leather straps was a strange contraption. On his front was a wooden box with a winding handle on one side, and two brass buttons and a knob on the front. A flexible metal tube connected the box to a pair of folded wings, made from leather, wood, and brass, on his back.

The boy slid the drain cover back into place, reached inside his under-suit and pulled out a toy figure dressed just like him. He held the doll out and spoke.

'Grandfather, I am up top. I think I'll have to go gardening tonight. It's a Sunday, and everything is shut. The bins behind the inn will be empty.'

There was a crackle of static, and a thin voice came from the doll. 'Well, you be careful, Arthur! And remember, only take from the bigger gardens . . . and only then if they have plenty! There are a lot of people that can only survive by growing their own food.'

Arthur smiled. He had heard this many times before. 'Don't worry, Grandfather, I haven't forgotten! I'll see you as soon as I'm done.'

Arthur replaced the doll inside his suit, then started to wind the handle on the box on his front. It made a soft whirring noise. For nearly two minutes he wound, pausing occasionally when his hand started aching. Then a bell pinged from somewhere inside the box and he stopped. Arthur scanned the skyline, crouched, and then pressed one of the buttons. The wings on his back unfolded. He pressed the other button while jumping as high as he could. Silently the wings caught the air as he leapt. At the bottom of their stroke they folded, rose, and then beat down again. His wings were holding him in the air, a few feet above the ground. Arthur's hand reached for the knob and he turned it just a little. As he did so he tilted himself forward. He started to move. Arthur smiled . . . he was flying.

He moved slowly down the lane, keeping below the top of its walls. When he reached the end, he adjusted the knob again, and rose up to a gap between the twin roofs of the Glue Factory. Arthur knew routes that were safe from the eyes of the townsfolk. When it was dark or there was thick smog, things were easy. But tonight was clear and the moon full. He'd been spotted twice before on nights like these, by children, from their bedroom windows. He'd got away with it so far, as nobody had believed them when they said they had seen a fairy or flying boy, but tonight he would not take any chances.

Arthur reached the end of the gap between the roofs. He dipped a little and flew across a large stable yard. A horse started and whinnied as he flew over. He adjusted his wing speed and increased his height. The horse made him feel uneasy. At the far side of the yard he rose again over a huge spiked gate. He crossed a deserted alley, then moved down a narrow street flanked with the windowless backs of houses. He came to another high wall. Carefully he adjusted the knob, and rose very gently to the point where he could just see the ground beyond the wall. It was a large vegetable garden, bathed in paths of pale light, cast from the windows of the house. Arthur saw one of the windows was open. From it he could hear raised voices and the clatter of dominoes.

That should keep them busy! he thought, scanning the garden again. Against the wall furthest from the house was a large glass lean-to.

He checked the house again, then rose over the wall and headed for the greenhouse, keeping above the beams of light from the windows. He came to rest in front of the greenhouse door, turning off and folding his wings.

He opened the door, and a soft rush of warm perfumed air brushed his face. It was a mixture of smells—some familiar, some not.

Dark leafy forms filled the greenhouse, suspended from the roof, others climbing almost invisible strings. As Arthur entered he recognized tomato plants, cucumbers, and grapes hanging from above.

He made his way to a tree against the far wall, a tree with branches only at its top. Dangling from a stem below the branches was a large bunch of bananas.

Arthur could hardly contain his delight. He tore a banana from the bunch, then peeled and ate it ravenously. When he had finished, he turned and checked the house. Nothing had changed. He reached inside his under-suit and took out a string bag, then pulled eagerly at the banana bunch. It was not as easy to pick the full bunch as it had been to pull off a single banana, and Arthur found he had to put his full weight on the bunch. Still it did not come down. In desperation, Arthur lifted his feet from the ground and swung his legs. All of a sudden there was a crack and the whole bunch, along with Arthur, fell to the ground. The tree trunk sprang back up and struck the glass roof with a loud smash.

'Oi! There is something in the greenhouse!' came a shout from the house.

Arthur scrambled to his feet, grabbed the string bag and looked out through the glass. No one was in the garden yet. He rushed to collect up as many of the bananas as possible, shoving them into the bag. Then he heard a door bang and the sound of footsteps. He ran out of the greenhouse into the garden.

Clambering towards him over the rows of vegetables was a very large lady with a very long stick. Arthur dashed over to one of the garden walls, stabbed at the buttons on the front of his box, and jumped. His wings snapped open and started to beat, but not strongly enough to lift him. He landed back on the ground. Arthur groaned—the bananas gave him extra weight! But he was not ready to put them down and fly away empty-handed—they were too precious. Still clutching the string bag in one hand, he grabbed for the knob on the front of the box with the other, and twisted it hard. The wings immediately doubled their beating and became a blur. Just as the woman reached the spot where Arthur stood, he shot almost vertically upwards. Furious, she swung her stick above her head and, before he could get out of range, landed a hard blow on his wings, sending him spinning.

'You little varmint! Give me back my bananas!' the woman cried.

Arthur grasped at the top of the wall to steady himself, adjusted the wings quickly, and made off over the wall.

Arthur felt sick to the pit of his stomach. Coming up at night to collect food was always risky, and this was the closest he'd ever been to being caught. He needed somewhere quiet to rest and recover.

I wish we could live above ground like everybody else! he thought.

Now he flew across the town by the safest route he knew—flying between roofs, up the darkest alleys, and across deserted yards—till finally he reached the abandoned Cheese Hall. He knew he would be alone here.

The Cheese Hall had been the grandest of all the buildings in the town and was only overshadowed by a few of the factory chimneys. In former times, it had been the home of the Ratbridge Cheese Guild. But now the industry was dead, and the Guild and all its members ruined. The Hall was now boarded up and deserted. Its gilded statues that once shone out across the town were blackened by the very soot that had poisoned the cheese.

Arthur landed on the bridge of the roof, and was settling himself amongst the statues when he heard a mournful bleat. He listened carefully, intrigued, but heard no more, so he stowed the bananas behind one of the statues, climbed out from his hiding place, and flew up to the plinth on the top of the roof that supported the weathervane and lightning conductor.

A complete panorama of the town and the surrounding countryside, broken only by the chimneystacks of the factories, was laid out before him. In the far distance he could just make out some sort of procession in the moonlight making for the woods. It looked as though something was being chased by a group of horses.

Chapter 2

The Hunt

Strange sounds were filtering through the woods—scrabblings, bleatings and growlings—and, strangest of all, a sound closely resembling bagpipes, or the sound bagpipes would make if they were being strangled, viciously, under a blanket. In a small moonlit clearing in the centre of the woods the sounds grew louder. Suddenly there was a frantic rustling in the bushes on one side of the clearing, and three large barrel cheeses broke from the undergrowth, running as fast as their legs would carry them. Hurtling across the clearing, bleating in panic, they disappeared into the bushes on the far side, and for a moment all was still again.

Suddenly a new burst of rustling came from the bushes where the cheeses had emerged, along with a horrid growling noise. Then a pack of hounds burst out into the open, all shapes and sizes. They ran around in circles, growling through their muzzles. One small fat animal that looked like a cross between a sausage dog and a ball of wire wool kept his nose to the ground, sniffing intently. He gave a great snort, crossed the clearing, and dived onwards after the cheeses. The other hounds followed.

The weird bagpipe sound grew closer, accompanied by vaguely human cries. Then there was a louder crashing in the undergrowth and finally the strangest creature yet arrived in the clearing. It had four skinny legs that hung from what looked like an upturned boat made from a patchwork of old sacking. At its front was a head made from an old box, and on this the features of a horse's face were crudely drawn. A large angry man rode high on its back.

'Which way did they go?' the man screamed.

An arm emerged from the sacking and pointed across the clearing. The rider took his horn and blew, filling the clearing with the horrible bagpipe-like sound. Then he raised the horn high in the air and brought it down hard on his steed.

'Hummgggiff Gummmminn Hoofff!' came muffled cries of pain from below.

The creature started to move in a wobbly line across the clearing, picking up speed as the rider beat it harder. More men on these strange creatures arrived, following the sound of the horn. They were just in time to catch the lead rider disappearing. They too beat their mounts. As they did, shouts of 'Tally-ho!' and 'Gee-up!' could be heard over the cries from the beasts below.

The front legs of the last of these creatures came to a sudden halt. However, the back legs kept moving and, inevitably, caught up with the front legs. There was an 'Ooof!' and a sweaty red face emerged from the front of the creature. The head looked up at the rider and spoke.

'That's it, Trout! I have had enough! I want a go on top.'

'But I only got a "turn" since the start of the woods, and you had a long go across the fields,' moaned the rider. Another face now emerged from the back end of the creature, and joined in.

'Yes! . . . and Gristle, you tried to make us jump that gate!'

'Well, I'm not going on, and I'll blame you two if we get in trouble for getting left behind,' said the face at the front.

'All right then!' the rider said with a pout.

He jumped down, and as he took off his jacket and top hat, the creature's body lifted to reveal two men underneath. The man at the front unstrapped himself, and the rider took his place. The body lowered itself and the new rider put on the jacket and hat, and climbed with some difficulty into the saddle.

'Don't you dare try going through the stream,' the back end of the creature demanded.

'All right, but make sure we catch up,' said the new rider. 'You know the rules about being last!'

The woods now disgorged a weird procession. First the cheeses, then after a few moments the hounds, followed by the huntsmen. Then the first of the cheese-hounds struck. One of the smaller cheeses was trailing a few yards behind the rest. It was an easy target. In one leap, the hound landed its front paws on the cheese. Whimpering and bleating, the cheese struggled to get free, but it was no good. Its legs buckled, and it collapsed on the grass.

Chapter 3

From on High

Arthur watched the cheese hunt from his perch on top of the Cheese Hall. He grabbed his doll from under his suit, and raised it to his mouth.

'Grandfather! Grandfather! It's Arthur. Can you hear me?' There was a crackling and his grandfather replied.

'Yes, Arthur, I can hear you. What's happening?'

'I think I can see a cheese hunt!'

There was a pause, then Grandfather spoke again. 'Are you sure? Cheese hunting is illegal. Where are you?'

'I am sitting on top of the Cheese Hall. I am . . . ' Arthur decided to gloss over earlier events, ' . . . having a break. I can see the whole thing. Riders and hounds chasing and catching cheeses.'

'But they can't! It's cruel, and illegal!' Grandfather sputtered. 'Are you sure there are riders on horses?'

'Yes, Grandfather. Although there's something rather odd about them.'

'What is it?'

'They're very ungainly, and somewhat oddly shaped . . .'

'Where are they now?' asked Grandfather.

'They are approaching the West Gate.'

'Well, they must be from the town then. If we could find out who was responsible, perhaps we could do something to put a stop to it. Do you think you could have a closer look without being seen?'

'Yes, I think so,' Arthur said, starting to feel excited.

'Well, keep up on the roofs, and see if you can follow them.' Grandfather paused. 'BUT . . . be very careful!'

'Don't worry, I will be. I'll call you as soon as I find out anything.'

Arthur put the doll away and wound his wings again.

Here at last was a chance for some real adventure.

Chapter 4

Into the Town

Arthur flew from the Cheese Hall to a rooftop near the West Gate, and settled out of sight behind a parapet. He looked down.

In the street below the hunt wove its way into town. It was a terrifying sight. Strange four-legged creatures were carrying very ugly men in very tall hats. A pack of manky hounds sniffed around behind them, and just visible in the shadows were short tubby yellow cheeses tied with pieces of string to some of the riders. One of these cheeses stumbled on the cobbles and let out a bleat.

'Quick!' hissed Snatcher. 'Muffle 'im! We don't want to get caught.'

A rider threw a large sack over the cheese and it fell silent.

Arthur moved along the parapet till he reached the end of the building. He pressed the buttons on the front of his box, rose silently and flew towards the next house. He was proud of himself—he had not made a single sound that had attracted their attention. But there was something wrong. He was losing height.

There was a snapping sound and he felt himself jerk to one side . . . then start to drop. The banana woman's stick must have damaged his wings. He was falling! Arthur grabbed for the knob and twisted it hard. Still he dropped. He looked around—his broken right wing was just dragging limply above him like a streamer. Meanwhile, the procession below had seen him. Snatcher was driving his mount towards the spot Arthur would fall. In a last desperate attempt, Arthur reached for the handle on the side of the box and started to wind for all he was worth. The remaining wing sped up. Harder and harder he wound. His descent slowed to a stop . . . just above Snatcher.

Still Arthur wound, harder and harder. Then he felt something grab his ankle. Arthur tried to pull away. There was a cackling from below.

''Ow ingenious! I always rather fancied flying,' came a voice.

'Let me go!' cried Arthur.

'I shall not!'

Arthur felt a sharp tug, swinging him around, and the

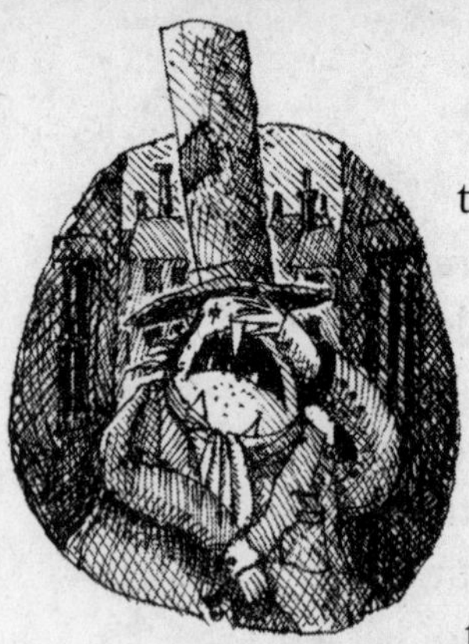

tip of his broken wing poked Snatcher straight in the left eye.

'Wwwwwwwwwwwwaaaaaaaaaa-aaaaaaahhhh!!' Snatcher cried, releasing his grip on Arthur's ankle and putting a hand to his eye. Arthur kept winding, kicking off from one of the walls and starting down the alley. Behind him he could hear a very pained Snatcher.

'Get the little tyke!' screamed Snatcher.

Though he kept winding, there was no way Arthur could get high enough to escape over the roofs—his damaged wing could barely keep him above the ground. To get back to the drain, he would have to make his way through the streets and alleys. But the cheese-hounds were now snapping below him . . .

Ahead of him the alley faded into darkness, and he turned through an archway into a yard beyond. With a start of relief, Arthur realized he knew where he was. The yard backed onto the lane where the drain—and the way home—was. He had a chance of getting there, if his wings would just hold out long enough. The wall dividing him from the lane was only a few feet higher than he was flying. He might just make it.

But the remaining wing could not take any more. With a sharp tearing noise, the leather tore away from the wing spars. Arthur frantically reached out for the wall, but it was no good. He was falling—and the cheese-hounds were waiting for him below. Dropping to the ground, he spun round to face the drooling hounds, bracing himself for the worst. But they held back, seeming to be a little scared by the flailing wing spar.

For a wild moment Arthur wondered if he could somehow beat them back, but then there was a crunching noise from the box and the skeleton of the last wing stopped. The hounds spread out in a circle around him, growling and snapping, looking for a chance to pounce. Desperately, Arthur tore one of the wing spars from his back, and spun around to confront any dog that seemed to be getting closer. He noticed a water butt in the corner of the yard. Perhaps if he could manage to get onto that, he might have a chance. Fending off the dogs, he moved towards the butt. The hounds moved with him.

Then Arthur's heart sank again. Snatcher had entered the yard. 'No you don't, you little vermin. I have plans for you! . . . And your wings.'

He walked towards Arthur, his eye now so swollen that it had closed.

Snatcher snarled and made a lunge for Arthur. Arthur jumped back, and bumped into the butt. He was completely cornered.

'Now, boy, give me those wings of yours. I am very interested in contraptions! Now!' Snatcher ordered.

Arthur slowly reached for the buckle on one of his shoulders.

'Faster, boy! Or I'll be setting the hounds on yer!'

Arthur released one buckle, then another and finally the last one at his side. Arthur slipped the wings over his head, and Snatcher grabbed at them.

'Clever, very clever . . . might well be useful!' Snatcher mused as he turned the remains of the wings over in his huge hands.

Arthur stood with his back against the water butt, glancing from the snapping dogs to Snatcher. Grandfather had warned him so many times about being careful. Now, having made just one mistake, he was in real trouble for the first time in his life.

Arthur slowly moved his hands back onto the butt then, stealthily, always keeping an eye on Snatcher, he pulled himself up till he was sitting on the edge of it. The hounds started to growl and strain forward, but Snatcher was so absorbed in the wings that he absent-mindedly shushed them. Arthur raised his knees till his heels were resting on the edge of the butt.

One of the hounds let out a bark then, and Snatcher looked up and realized what was happening. He let out a cry of rage just as Arthur jumped up, turned, grabbed the top of the wall and pulled himself over it.

He fell flat to the ground on the other side, and winded himself. He lay for a few seconds trying to catch his breath, listening to the shouts of anger and barking from over the wall.

'Get round the back and 'ave 'im!' Snatcher bellowed. There was the sound of leather on dog and then a loud howling.

Arthur scrambled to his feet and started for the drain cover at the far end of the lane, but he wasn't going to make it. He ducked into a doorway in the wall, then peeped back out. Snatcher, surrounded by hounds, stood right by the drain cover. There were more footsteps and the rest of the riders appeared.

'I think he went down here! Must live down below! Go and get the glue and an iron plate!' Snatcher ordered. A group of the hunters disappeared.

Snatcher turned and scanned the alley. 'OK, the rest of you search the alley, just in case.'

The men stood for a moment while the hounds sniffed the air. Then the little dog that looked like a cross between a sausage dog and a ball of wire wool started to make his way down the alley directly towards Arthur. Arthur pressed his back against the door, shivering with fear. This time there really was no way out.

Suddenly he felt the door give way behind him. Something grabbed him around the knees, pulled him through the doorway, and the door slammed shut.

Chapter 5

Here Be Monsters!

Arthur found himself standing in total darkness. The overwhelming relief at having got away from Snatcher and his hounds was mixed with the awful fear that he might have been dragged into something even worse. Who or what had pulled him through that door and why? A soft gurgling noise came from somewhere behind him. He turned round towards it, and trod on something. There was a squeak, a scuffling of feet, and the sound of a doorknob being turned. Light broke in as a door opened. It framed a boxtroll, its smiling head protruding from its large cardboard box.

Arthur had seen boxtrolls before, underground, occasionally coming across them as he explored the dark passages, caverns, and tunnels. Boxtrolls were timid creatures and always scuttled away as soon as they noticed his presence. This was the first time Arthur had seen one close at hand.

Arthur walked towards the smiling, beckoning boxtroll hesitantly. It turned and scampered up a huge heap of nuts and bolts that covered the floor of the room ahead. As it reached the top, it stopped and picked up a handful of the nuts and bolts, lifting them to its mouth and kissing them. It then sprinkled them back over the heap, and grinned at him. Arthur knew that boxtrolls loved everything mechanical. They did a lot of maintenance work underground, draining the passages, and shoring up the tunnels and caves.

Arthur clambered over the heap and followed the boxtroll into a small hallway. Ahead of them was a panelled door through which a warm yellow light shone. The boxtroll knocked on the door.

'Come on in, Fish!' a muffled voice replied.

The boxtroll turned again to Arthur and smiled. Then it opened the door, walked a few steps into the room, and cleared its throat.

'Well, what is it, Fish?' A man's voice came from somewhere inside the room. 'What treasures have you brought to show us this evening? Let's have a look!'

The boxtroll reached for Arthur's hand and led him into the room.

Arthur's jaw fell open. From amongst the cages, tanks, boxes, old sofas, clocks, brass bedstead, piles of straw, and heaps of books, stared four pairs of eyes. There were two more boxtrolls sitting on a shelf, a small man with a cabbage tied to the top of his head, and an old man sitting in a huge high-backed leather armchair. He was wearing half glasses and a grey wig, and was smiling at Arthur.

'Hello. Who do we have here?'

Arthur blinked. The old man waited patiently.

'I'm Arthur!' he finally said.

'Well, Arthur, are you a friend of Fish?' the old man asked.

The two other boxtrolls made spluttering noises. The boxtroll holding Arthur's hand turned to him, squeezed his hand, and made a happy gurgling sound.

'Yes,' said the old man, 'I think you are!' He looked sternly at the two boxtrolls on the shelf. 'And Shoe and Egg should know better than to snigger at Fish!' The two boxtrolls fell silent, their faces turning bright red.

The room was packed to overflowing. If you took a junk shop, added the contents of a small zoo, then threw all your household possessions on top, it would start to give you an idea of what it was like. It smelt a little of compost. But it was warm and quiet, everyone looked friendly, and—best of all—there were no hounds snapping at him.

Somehow, he felt safe. Safe enough to ask a question.

'Please, sir, may I ask you who you are?' asked Arthur.

'Certainly, young man!' the old man grinned. 'I am Willbury Nibble QC . . . Retired! I was a lawyer, but now I live here with my companions. This was a pet shop, but now I rent it to live in. And these are my friends.' Willbury looked around at the creatures. 'You have met Fish already it would seem, and these two reprobates,' he nodded at the other boxtrolls, 'are Shoe and Egg.'

The boxtrolls on the shelf smiled at Arthur. Then the old man turned to the little man with the cabbage on his head. 'And this is Titus. He is a cabbagehead.' Titus scurried behind the old man's chair.

'I am afraid he is rather nervous. He'll get used to you, though, and then you will find him charming.'

A cabbagehead! Grandfather had told Arthur stories about cabbageheads. Legend had it that they lived in the caverns deep underground. It was said that they grew strange vegetables there, and worshipped cabbages. Even Grandfather had not seen a cabbagehead, they were so shy.

Arthur thought for a moment then asked, 'Your friends are all underlings, so why do they live with you?'

Willbury smiled. 'What do you know about underlings, Arthur?'

'I know that the boxtrolls look after the tunnels and plumbing underground,' said Arthur.

'Well, our boxtroll friends here act as scouts, though I'm not sure I entirely approve.' Willbury gave the boxtrolls a funny look.

'Scouts?' asked Arthur.

'Yes. Boxtrolls have a need for certain supplies to help with their maintenance of the Underworld. So Fish, Shoe, and Egg wander the town looking for "supplies"! When they find them they "prepare" the item for removal—loosen it, unbolt it, unscrew it, whatever. That's why there is such a large heap of nuts and bolts in the back room. God help me if I was ever visited by the police. They leave signs for the other boxtrolls, strange chalk marks on the walls about town to guide the other boxtrolls to the "supplies" so they can make a quick getaway!'

Arthur looked across at Fish, who grinned and nodded.

'Yes,' said Willbury, rather sternly. 'Our friends the boxtrolls have a rather strange attitude towards ownership. Have you not noticed that most of your arrows point at someone else's property?'

The boxtrolls looked rather guilty. Arthur felt a little guilty himself remembering the bananas he had left on top of the Cheese Hall.

'Titus here is researching gardening,' Willbury continued. 'The cabbageheads are always trying to improve their methods of cultivation. So occasionally one of them spends some time up here studying human gardening methods. Egg and Shoe discovered Titus one night sleeping in a coalbunker and brought him back. He's been here for a few weeks writing up a report on gardening. When he's finished he will go back to the Underworld.'

A squeak of agreement came from behind the chair, though Titus kept hidden behind it.

'Now, Arthur, please sit down, and tell me what brings you here.' Willbury lifted his feet from a footstool, and pushed it towards Arthur.

Arthur suddenly felt overwhelmed. He didn't know where to begin. Fish came forward, and started talking.

'Hummif gommmong shoegger tooff!!!'

'I think it would be better if Arthur explained himself, Fish,' said Willbury. He smiled encouragingly at Arthur. 'Are you in trouble?'

'Yes,' whispered Arthur.

'Well, let's hear what kind of trouble it is. We'll try to help you if we can. I have spent my whole life trying to sort out trouble for other people.'

Arthur hesitated, then decided he could trust Willbury. 'Yes, I am in trouble. I live underground with Grandfather . . . and now they've blocked my hole back.

It's the only way I know to get home . . . And they have taken my wings!' Speaking the words aloud made Arthur realize fully what a terrible situation he was in. Would he ever be able to get back to Grandfather?

Willbury looked concerned. 'I think you had better tell me the full story.'

'I'm from the Underworld . . . well, I have lived there since I was a baby.'

'You live underground?'

'Yes . . . Me and my grandfather live in a cave . . . well, three caves actually. One we use as a living room and kitchen, another is Grandfather's bedroom and workshop, and the smallest is mine. It's my bedroom. It's warm and cosy, a bit like this place.'

'But why do you live underground?' Willbury asked in a puzzled voice.

'I'm . . . I'm not really sure. Grandfather always tells me he'll explain when I'm older.'

'And what about your parents?'

Arthur looked sad. 'I don't know . . .'

'But your grandfather?'

'Oh . . . He's not my real grandfather, he just found me abandoned on the steps of the workhouse, when I was a baby, and took me back to live with him. He's raised me like he was my father, but because he's so much older I call him "Grandfather".'

'So has he always lived underground?'

Arthur thought for a moment. 'No, he said he lived in the town when he was younger . . . But he doesn't talk about it . . . '

Willbury decided to change the subject a little. 'You say "they" have blocked your hole back to the underground and taken your wings? Who is "they"?'

Arthur spoke mournfully. 'I saw these men hunting cheese and I went to have a look, but my wings broke and the hunters took them and then I escaped, and was trying to get back down underground when they blocked up my hole.'

'But what were you doing above ground?'

Arthur's face grew red. 'I was gathering food. It's the only way we can survive. My grandfather is so frail now that I have to do it. And he made me some wings so I could get about the town easily.'

'Your grandfather made you wings?'

'Yes, he can make anything. He made my doll as well so I could talk to him while I am above ground.' Arthur reached inside his under-suit and pulled out the doll to show Willbury.

Willbury's eyes grew wide. 'Does it still work?'

'Yes . . . I think so.' Arthur looked at the doll closely—it didn't look damaged.

'When did you last speak to your grandfather?'

'An hour or so ago.'

'Does he know what's happened to you or where you are?'

'No . . . ' said Arthur.

'Well, I suggest you speak to your grandfather right now to let him know you are all right, and that you are here! And when you have spoken to your grandfather, I should like to talk to him, if I may?' asked Willbury.

Arthur nodded. He wound the tiny handle on the box on the front of the doll. There was a gentle crackling noise, and then Grandfather's voice broke through.

'Arthur, Arthur, are you out there?'

'Yes! Yes! It's me! Grandfather, it's me! Arthur!' Arthur yelped. It was such a relief to hear Grandfather's voice.

'Arthur! Where are you? I've been so worried. Are you all right?' Grandfather's voice sounded shaky.

'I did try to be careful, Grandfather, but the cheese huntsmen tried to catch me . . . They took my wings! And sealed up the drain hole! But I'm safe now! I'm in an old shop, with a man called Willbury. He wants to speak to you.'

'Certainly—please pass the doll to him.' Arthur gave the doll to Willbury, who had been looking at it a little uneasily. Willbury cleared his throat.

'Good evening, sir. This is Willbury Nibble speaking. I have Arthur with me in my home. I haven't heard the full story, but it sounds as if he has had a terrible time. You have my word as a gentleman, that while your grandson is in my charge I shall do all within my

power to keep him safe. I shall also endeavour to help him return to you, as soon as maybe!'

'Thank you, Mr Nibble!' replied Grandfather. 'If you could help Arthur get back to me safely, I would be very grateful!'

Arthur moved closer to the doll. 'Grandfather, how am I going to get back now that the huntsmen have blocked up the drain?'

'I know there are other routes between the town and the Underworld. But I don't know where they are. They belong to other creatures.' Grandfather's voice sounded sad.

'Sir,' replied Willbury, 'I have a number of boxtrolls and a cabbagehead living with me. They may know of a way!'

Willbury looked up and was met by nodding heads. Even Titus had come out of hiding and was nodding.

'Yes! It seems they do,' said Willbury. 'I will have them help us guide Arthur back to you!'

'Thank you!' came the voice from the doll.

Arthur looked at the creatures gratefully. Of course—it was such a simple answer. He needn't have been so worried. Then Willbury spoke again.

'I suggest we wait till early tomorrow morning—these blackguards who chased Arthur will be gone by then—and Fish and the others can find Arthur a hole.'

'I agree, Mr Nibble. I think Arthur has had enough excitement for one evening. Getting Arthur back is my first concern. But I am worried about his wings. Without them he won't be able to collect food for us safely . . . '

'I understand your concern, sir. Let me think on it. It's getting late now, so I suggest that we all get some sleep. Do you have enough food for the moment?' asked Willbury.

'Yes, I have several large clumps of rhubarb, growing under the bed,' said Grandfather.

'Good. We'll give Arthur a good supper, and there is plenty of space for him to sleep here.'

'Thank you so much, Mr Nibble. And Arthur, look after yourself . . . I need you back!' said Grandfather.

'I will, Grandfather. Goodnight,' replied Arthur.

'Goodnight, Arthur, and I shall see you in the morning.'

Willbury made up a bed for Arthur under the shop counter, out of old velvet curtains.

'You sleep well, Arthur. I have an idea where we might make enquiries about your wings.'

Arthur pulled the soft velvet covers over his head. The curtain felt heavy and gave off rather a comforting dusty smell. Arthur lay quietly in the darkness and started to think. About getting back to Grandfather, and his wings.

His thoughts became slower as sleep overtook him. Soon all that could be heard was gentle snoring.

Chapter 6

Search for a Hole

Arthur woke up with a start. He sat up and banged his head on the wooden shelf above him. Then he remembered where he was. Pale daylight filled the space between the counter and the wall behind it. A face popped into view, and smiled at him.

'Good morning, Fish!' Arthur said, rubbing his head.

After Willbury had made them a breakfast of cocoa porridge, the group made its way through the back streets of Ratbridge, the boxtrolls taking the lead. At each corner they checked for humans, then waved the group on. As yet they had the town to themselves.

Within ten minutes they were approaching the site of Fish's hole. They'd decided to try his first, because they could reach it via alleys and small pathways—hopefully without being seen.

Fish had stopped by a door in a garden wall.

He signed to the others to keep quiet and follow him. He pushed at the door and they all made their way into an overgrown garden—clearly the house was deserted. Fish led them to a brick outhouse, and opened its door. Then he let out an anguished squeak.

The others crowded round to see what had upset him. A large rusty iron plate covered the floor inside. Some kind of dried black glue bulged from around its edges.

Fish turned to them and started to make gobbling noises.

'Confound it!' said Willbury. 'Let's see if we can lift it. We could try to force something under the edge.'

Arthur spotted an old spade in the brambles, and hurried to fetch it. Willbury smiled.

'Good thinking, Arthur. I think Fish is the strongest one here. Give him the spade, and let him try.'

Fish tried to push it under the edge of the iron plate. But the glue was so hard that even after a great deal of effort he made no impression.

'I don't think we should worry too much, Fish. The hole must have been found when someone was doing repairs on the house, and they just covered it up,' said Willbury consolingly. 'Let's try another hole.'

Fish frowned. He threw the spade down in a rather bad-tempered way.

'Fish! That is not the sort of behaviour I expect from a boxtroll. Pick that up and leave it neatly against the wall, please,' Willbury said sternly.

Fish looked huffy, but did what he was told.

'Shoe, I think your hole is the closest one to here. Let's go there.' Willbury put his hand on Arthur's shoulder. 'Don't worry. We'll have you back home before you can say Jack Robinson.'

The group passed through a few more empty streets, then arrived outside a butcher's shop. Shoe led them up the side alley next to the shop, and into a walled yard. On one side was a derelict pigsty. Shoe looked about, then opened the pigsty's gate and went inside. He came back out looking worried. He took Willbury's hand, and led him into the sty. Arthur and the others followed. Old straw had been pushed up around the edges of the sty revealing another large iron plate.

'Oh dear!' muttered Willbury. 'This looks bad. Two holes both sealed up!'

'Three if you count mine,' said Arthur.

'You're right, Arthur. This seems more than a coincidence,' said Willbury, sounding worried.

Arthur was also starting to feel worried. He took a long look at the iron plate. 'This is how the huntsmen sealed up my hole last night.' Suddenly getting home did not seem so straightforward after all.

'We had better go and check the other holes forthwith,' said a perturbed Willbury.

Egg gurgled to Willbury.

'Yes, Egg! Let's check your hole. Hopefully we'll have more luck there.'

They left the pigsty and emerged up the alley onto the street. A few people were now out and about, pushing handcarts towards the market. They didn't seem to pay any attention to Arthur, Willbury, and the creatures, but the boxtrolls looked uneasy, and Titus nervously tried to keep Arthur between himself and the humans.

Egg led them to a rubbish heap behind the Glue Works, where he immediately started pulling pieces of junk away from one end of the heap. After a few moments he stopped, turned, and looked back at them. The boxtrolls started to make an agitated mewing sound. Willbury and Arthur and could see sunlight glinting off an iron plate.

'Why would anyone do this?' Arthur asked.

'I am not sure . . . but I have got a very bad feeling about it. We should check Titus's hole, even though it's too small for you to fit through.'

The group set off at a real pace this time. The streets

were now filling but Arthur noticed that nobody seemed to take much notice of boxtrolls, yet they still seemed nervous and kept to the shadows. Titus moved more and more quickly, so concerned about getting to his hole that he hardly noticed the humans around him. Then he disappeared around a corner into an alley. The others turned the corner to see Titus in the distance, running towards a drain. Before he reached it, he stopped.

The others caught up, to find Titus whimpering to himself next to an iron-covered hole. For several seconds no one said a word.

Finally, Willbury spoke. 'I'm so sorry, Arthur, but I am not sure what I can do. This is terrible . . .' He turned to the underlings. Do you know of any more holes?'

The underlings slowly shook their heads.

Willbury gazed at the iron cover for a while then spoke. 'I really have no idea what is going on. I think it best if we all go back to the shop.'

He started to walk back up the path. The others followed in silence. As they trailed through the now crowded streets, Titus gripped Arthur's hand. Things did not look good.

Chapter 7

The Return

As soon as they were inside the shop Willbury turned to Arthur. 'I think we had better call your grandfather. He needs to know what's going on.' Arthur nodded in agreement.

They didn't stay on the phone for long. Arthur explained the problems with the holes, and Willbury told his grandfather that he knew someone in the world of inventions who might be able to help.

It was near the end of the conversation when Willbury looked quizzical and said, 'If you don't mind me asking—why do you live underground?'

There was a long pause. When Grandfather finally replied, there was a steely tone to his voice that Arthur had never heard before. 'I was accused of a crime that I did not commit. I have had to take refuge here ever since.'

Arthur felt his skin prickle. This was the closest he had ever come to finding out the reason for their life underground. Would Grandfather say more? What sort of crime could have driven him underground for so long?

'I have kept it from Arthur as I felt he was too young to understand,' his grandfather continued. 'But please believe me when I say you have my word as a gentleman that I am an innocent man.'

'I believe you, sir,' said Willbury. Then, looking at Arthur, he spoke again. 'We shall leave it at that. I think it better he hears this sort of thing from you face to face.'

'Thank you,' came the voice from the doll.

Willbury looked at Arthur one more time, then asked another question. 'On a more immediate matter. Do you have enough food?'

'Yes. The rhubarb seems to be thriving. I think I have a few days' supply.'

'Well, hopefully we can get this matter sorted out very quickly. We will go and see my friend this morning. I am sure she will be able to help,' said Willbury. 'I will

make sure that Arthur calls you as soon as we have any information.'

'Thank you . . . And, Arthur, YOU TAKE CARE . . . I need you back.'

'All right, Grandfather!' said Arthur. He took the doll from Willbury. 'I will be very careful . . . and I will be back . . . Soon!'

Arthur was trying to sound positive, but actually he felt very unsure now of when he was going to get home—if ever.

'Right!' said Willbury firmly. 'I think we need a good feed. I can always think better on a full stomach. Let's draw up a shopping list.'

Arthur could tell that Willbury was as worried as he was, but that he was trying to keep everyone's spirits up. If he could put a brave face on the situation, then Arthur would too. He tried to raise a smile as they all sat down around the shop. Willbury took out a quill and a scrap of paper from under his chair.

Then there was a knock.

Chapter 8
A Visit

Everyone turned to the door. Through the window they could see the tall shadow of a figure standing outside.

Willbury put his finger to his mouth. 'Quiet!' he whispered. 'It may be the hunters looking for Arthur. Arthur, quick, hide behind the counter.'

Arthur obeyed without hesitation. He never wanted to see the huntsmen again if he could help it. He got back down into the space where he had slept the night before. There was a crack in the woodwork, and by placing his eye close to it he could still see the shop door. He watched as Willbury unlocked the door and stepped back.

A rather grubby man wearing a frock coat and a top hat stood on the doorstep holding a large box in his arms.

'Excuse me, sir,' he said in an oily voice. 'My name is Gristle, and I represent the Northgate Miniature Livestock Company. I was wondering if you might be interested in buying some rather small creatures?'

Willbury looked quizzically at the box. 'Er. Umm. You know this is not a pet shop any more?' he said slowly. 'What are they?'

'They are the very latest thing! Miniatures! Little versions of some of the pet industry's best sellers.'

Mr Gristle put down the box and, with a flourish, took off the lid. Willbury couldn't help smiling.

'They're beautiful!' he said, squatting down. Then he frowned. 'But they don't seem very happy.'

'No,' replied Gristle. 'I think it's a by-product of the breeding.' He glanced at the underlings who'd moved shyly closer to have a look. 'You wouldn't like to do a swap, would you? I'm looking for BIG creatures,' Gristle said, eyeing up Willbury's companions. The underlings quickly hid behind Willbury.

'Certainly not!' Willbury blurted, outraged. 'How much do you want for them?'

'How would five groats sound?' said Gristle, rather hopefully.

'It would sound very expensive!' replied Willbury.

'Well, three groats, five farthings. It's my last offer. I can always take them to the pie shop,' Gristle smirked.

Willbury looked shocked, took out his leather coin bag and gave Gristle the money.

'Thank you, squire! Are you sure you don't want to part with any of your BIG friends?' Gristle asked again.

'Absolutely not! Now, be off with you!' Willbury had taken a distinct dislike to Mr Gristle. He closed the door on the salesman.

The letterbox flipped open.

'I really am very interested in your BIG friends, sir. I'm sure we could come to some arrangement?'

'Go AWAY!' said Willbury, starting to get angry.

The letterbox closed for a moment, and then a ten groat banknote appeared, held by two long thin grubby fingers.

'Pretty please,' whispered Gristle.

The fingers started to wave the note. Willbury took a lone cucumber from the vegetable box that was kept on the floor.

'I'm warning you. GO AWAY! I do not sell friends!' Willbury was turning red.

'Oh, go on! They are only dumb old underlings,' the voice said.

This was too much for Willbury. He raised the cucumber and brought it down on the letterbox flap. There was a 'Splut!' as the cucumber hit the flap, a 'Snap!' as the flap closed on the fingers, and a scream from outside. The fingers and the banknote disappeared.

A silence fell over the shop. Willbury turned and spoke. 'You can come out now, Arthur.'

Arthur joined the group huddled around the box. He peered inside. The bottom was covered with straw, with half a turnip, covered in tiny bite marks, lying in one corner. Standing amongst the straw were a number of tiny creatures, shaking with fear. There was a cabbagehead and a boxtroll, both about five inches high, and three trotting badgers. Most trotting badgers were the size of large dogs, but these were the size of mice.

Fish leant over the box, and made a low, cooing noise. The tiny boxtroll looked up and started squeaking. Fish looked puzzled. He looked up at Shoe and Egg, who also seemed puzzled. It was obviously a boxtroll, but they couldn't understand what it was saying. Shoe grunted softly. Fish nodded, raced out of the room, then raced back in again. In his hand was a brass nut and bolt. He laid them in the straw next to the tiny boxtroll, who made some more squeaking sounds, then picked up the nut and bolt, kissed them and gave them a hug. The big boxtrolls smiled.

'Now we must find homes for our new friends,' Willbury said. 'I want Fish, Shoe, and Egg to look after the little boxtroll, and Titus, you can look after the tiny cabbagehead.'

The big boxtrolls looked very happy. Willbury picked up the little boxtroll (who was still hugging the nut and bolt) and passed him to Fish. The other boxtrolls crowded around, cooing, and finally they set off around the shop to give their new friend a tour.

Titus looked nervous. Willbury lifted the tiny cabbagehead up to his nose. He took a sniff and smiled, then offered it to Titus to smell. Titus leant forward and took a tiny sniff.

After a moment a smile spread over his face too. He then lowered his face to the tiny cabbagehead and allowed it to smell him. The tiny cabbagehead gave a little squeak, and jumped onto Titus's shoulder.

'Why don't you show him where you live?' suggested Willbury.

Titus's eyes grew bright. He clutched the tiny cabbagehead to his chest, shot across the room, and disappeared through the hole in his barrel.

Willbury smiled. 'Titus really needed a companion!'

Suddenly there was a scuffling from the box and the trotting badgers scurried across the floor and disappeared into a mouse hole in the skirting board.

'Oh dear!' said Willbury.

Arthur picked up the box and turned it over. One corner had been chewed away, leaving a small hole.

'That's the problem with trotting badgers! They are really wild . . . and have REALLY sharp teeth,' said Arthur. 'I feel sorry for those mice . . . trotting badgers will eat anything.'

'Well, we'll leave out some milk and biscuits for them later. Maybe if we keep them fed they'll leave the mice alone. I don't think there is anything else we can do,' said Willbury.

The boxtrolls returned from their tour.

'How are you getting on with your new friend?' Willbury asked them.

Fish gurgled and pointed at a matchbox on the mantelpiece, then at the little boxtroll who Shoe was now holding.

'Oh! You have called him "Match". How very appropriate,' said Willbury.

The boxtrolls and Arthur giggled.

'Right, we had better get off to the market. I think it best if we leave the underlings and their new friends here.'

As Willbury opened the door, Arthur suddenly felt rather frightened. He'd never been outside during the day before.

'Keep close, I don't want to lose you,' said Willbury.

And off they set.

What they failed to notice was that across the street were three men in top hats and mufflers, sitting on a large cart. As Willbury and Arthur headed towards the market, the men climbed down. One lifted a large metal bar from the back of the cart. The other two took out some old sacks. The men then walked shiftily towards the shop, all the time checking to see that nobody was watching them.

Chapter 9

The Market

Willbury led Arthur through the streets of Ratbridge towards the market. Arthur had never been anywhere so crowded. There were tradesmen and women, farmers, shopkeepers, dogs, chickens, pigs, street sellers, buskers, and more children than he had ever seen in his life. The children took no notice of him as they played. Some of them were kicking a leather ball the size of a cabbage about, while others were chasing each other, or fiddling with sticks in puddles. Arthur felt a little jealous.

'Willbury?' asked Arthur. 'Yes, Arthur?'

'What do children do?'

'You know. Play with friends, and go to school, and the like . . .'

Arthur was not sure he did know. He looked at the children. 'I don't think I have any friends.'

Willbury stopped and turned to him. 'I think you do! What about Fish . . . and Egg and Shoe . . . and Titus . . . and me?'

Arthur smiled, and they walked on. It was so noisy! Approaching the market the streets became more and more crowded. Arthur found it very exciting. As they entered the market square they were met by a wall of rather shabby people.

'Hang on very tightly to my hand, Arthur!' said Willbury as he pushed into the throng.

Arthur grabbed Willbury's hand. Slowly they squeezed their way through the jostling mass of bodies. Arthur could see very little except when there was a break in the crowd and for a moment he would catch sight of the stalls . . . He was amazed! He had never seen such a profusion of things. Stacks of sausages, bundles of new and second-hand clothes, strange tools and gadgets, bottles of grim-looking medicines, stacks of broken furniture, toys, clocks, pots and pans . . . Even when he couldn't see much about him the smells kept flooding into his nostrils. Some were familiar, some new, some sweet, and some very, very unpleasant. Arthur felt boggled by it all. How strange the town seemed by day. Occasionally Willbury would guide them towards a stall where he would buy food, and then off they would set again on their journey.

Willbury finally declaring he'd finished with the shopping, they set off across the market in the direction of the Patent Hall, Arthur trying to keep up with Willbury as they pushed their way through the crowds. As they reached the edge of the market the crowds became even denser until finally they could no longer find their way through, and were forced to come to a stop.

They were in the middle of a large crowd of ladies who were cackling loudly, their bottoms wobbling in rhythm. Arthur had not seen bottoms like these before. From the way the ladies paraded their 'derrières' it seemed that to have an interesting behind was very much the thing! Round ones, cone-shaped ones, pyramidal ones, cuboid ones, and some that defied description. All large, and wobbling like jellies.

The ladies kept taking furtive looks at the competing behinds.

'Hark at her,' one lady said to another.

'Which one do you mean? That Ms Fox?' replied the other.

'Yes! Coming on hoity-toity with her new hexagonal buttocks,' said the first, with more than a hint of jealousy.

'No? And on shoes like that! She thinks she's the bee's knees, and she doesn't even realize that hessian went out weeks ago!'

Arthur had no idea what they were talking about. But they seemed to be in a state of high excitement. It was soon clear there was something unusual going on.

'What do you think is happening?' Arthur had to raise his voice to make himself heard above the rising sound of chattering and twittering.

'I am not sure. There's a platform with someone on,' Willbury called back.

He guided Arthur in front of him. The crowd parted a little and Arthur could see a high wooden platform. On it stood a very strange woman. She wore a dress that looked as if it was made from skinned sofa and cardboard, an enormous pink wig, and a pair of rubber gauntlets. She also had a patch over one eye.

'Who is it?' asked Arthur. Despite never having seen a woman dressed in such a way before, Arthur felt the woman was oddly familiar, but he couldn't work out where from.

The woman standing next to them overheard Arthur's question. 'Don't you know? It's Madame Froufrou . . . the fashion princess!'

Willbury and Arthur looked at each other, shrugged their shoulders, and turned back to watch.

The strange woman raised her arms to quiet the crowd and the din died down. The ladies of the town were now all aquiver, and some let out squeals of delight.

'I heard she's got something really special . . . and totally new,' whispered one.

'I can hardly bear it,' said another. 'I missed out last week and they haven't let me in the tea rooms since.'

A large wooden box was slid up onto the stage and the woman started to speak.

'Today, my little fashion friends, Madame Froufrou 'as a real treat for you.'

Little cries of 'Magnifique!' 'Wunderbar!' 'I must have one' 'I must have two' came from the crowd.

The lady on the platform gave a smirk. She leant over to the box, opened a door in its lid, and reached in with her large rubber-gloved hand. She paused, then looked about the crowd, and gave them a look of delight.

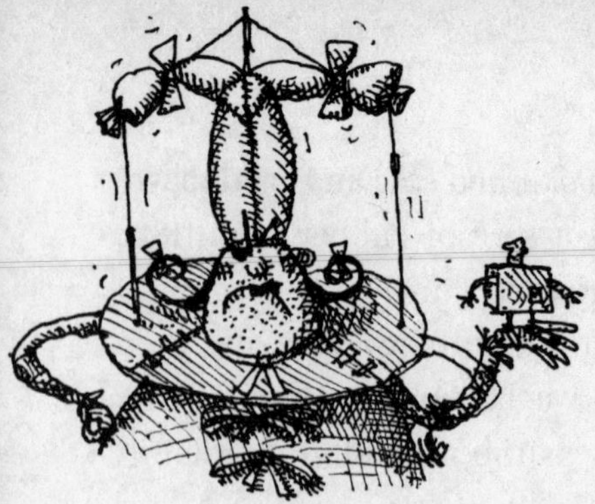

Then slowly she pulled out a tiny creature. It was a miniature boxtroll.

The crowd let out a gasp of admiration. Arthur turned to Willbury.

'It's just like the ones Gristle brought to the shop! What do you think is going on?' asked Arthur, shocked.

'I am not sure, but I don't like it!' replied Willbury.

Madame Froufrou started to speak again. ''Ere I 'ave a lickle lap creature, just the very sort the finest ladies of Pari are clamouring for as we speak. I 'ave a very limited supply.'

She paused and stared at the crowd. A soft pitiful moaning started all around.

'I cannot 'elp this, but it is for you to decide whether you are a woman of tomorrow or merely a ugly frump . . . with no sense of taste . . . or chance of social position!'

At this the ladies of the town started a desperate squeaking. Then someone cried: 'Me, me, sell one to me!'

Others immediately joined in the cry. 'ME, ME, Me, No! Me, ME!'

The noise grew so loud that Arthur had to put down his shopping and put his hands over his ears.

Madame Froufrou raised a hand. The cries halted and all that could be heard was the snapping of opening purses, and coins being counted.

'I cannot be kind to you all . . . My supplies are very limited.'

Someone in the audience let out a miserable whimper.

'So I think I shall do as they do in Pari,' said Madame Froufrou. 'I shall do what is the latest thing . . . and select only from those who are . . . fashionably . . . RICH!'

Several ladies in the crowd fainted.

Madame Froufrou scanned the crowd. 'Now, there is a question you must ask yourselves. Am I fashionably RICH? If you are not . . . you must cast yourself from this world of glamour and retire to your true miserable and rightfully low position.' She glowered at the crowd.

There was silence for a moment then cries of 'I am rich! I am rich! I am rich!'

Again Madame Froufrou raised her hand and silence returned.

'What a joy it is to be in such fashionable company. But . . . I have a feeling that hiding amongst us are some . . . DOWDY FRUMPS!'

The women around Arthur started to tremble with fear.

Madame Froufrou paused a long time for dramatic effect, then spoke again. 'I shall have to weed them out . . . BUT HOW?' There was another very long pause as she peered around the crowd. 'I have an idea . . . an idea that will show up the dowdy frumps hiding amongst us!' Several more ladies in the crowd fainted.

'Could the fashionable ladies here please raise their hands and display the most fashionable quantities of money they can!'

For a few moments all that could be heard was the rustling of banknotes and clinking of coins. Then hundreds of hands shot up and started to wave money. The ladies looked nervously around. Madame Froufrou took out an enormous pair of binoculars and started to scan the crowd.

'As I look at you all, I am shocked that one whole area is obviously harbouring the dowdy trying to pass themselves off as fashionable . . . I shall turn my back for a moment and let them crawl away . . . for if they are still here when I turn back . . . I shall POINT THEM OUT!' With that she turned her back.

The ladies now struggled to find every last penny to hold up in an attempt to avoid being labelled a frump.

Madame Froufrou turned slowly back and smiled. 'Ah! I see they have fled! It is only the stylish that remain. It is time for us to impart the new and ultimate accessory upon those who deserve it! Come hither, Roberto and Raymond.'

Two men dressed in dirty pink suits climbed onto the stage.

'These are my French fashion specialists and they are here to help me select those who are the most fashionable. Roberto and Raymond, please take out your fashion scopes and wands . . . Divine those that are expectable!'

Roberto and Raymond pulled out what looked like binoculars made from toilet rolls, and fishing rods with small buckets hung on the end. Looking through their binoculars they started to scan the crowd.

Roberto's gaze fixed upon a particularly full hand. 'Madame, I think I see a fashion angel,' he said, indicating the 'angel' in the crowd.

'Yes, it is true! A woman of grace and virtue! Now my angel, if you would place your offering in the bucket, and take a numbered ticket, I shall invite you to collect your very precious new lifestyle accessory from the stage, and lo . . . You shall be a queen amongst women!'

Roberto swung his wand out over the crowd to the angel's outstretched arm. The woman pushed all of her money into the bucket, took the ticket, and squeaked as she made her way towards the stage. Looks of hatred and envy followed her. Madame Froufrou passed the tiny boxtroll down to the angel in exchange for the ticket.

Roberto and Raymond began selecting more members of the crowd and exchanging tickets for cash, while Madame Froufrou stood by the wooden box and collected the tickets, and handed out more miniature boxtrolls. The crowd of ladies rapidly thinned.

Madame Froufrou looked around again and saw Arthur. For a moment she fixed him with a rather steely gaze, before turning her eye back on the ladies.

'Willbury, there is something about her. I get the feeling that I have met her before,' Arthur muttered nervously.

'And from the look of it, I think she thinks she knows you!' Willbury replied.

'I'm not sure where I could have seen her before. I know it's strange, but I got the same feeling when I was looking at her, that I got when the leader of the cheese hunt cornered me. She could have been his twin sister.'

'Very strange . . . ' Willbury paused to think. 'Something is very wrong . . . And weird. I think we had better go and find Marjorie. Maybe she can throw some light on things.'

Chapter 10
The Patent Hall

Willbury and Arthur made their way up the side streets towards the Patent Hall, and as they went they talked.

'Before today I'd never seen, nor even heard of, miniature boxtrolls, cabbageheads, or trotting badgers. And now miniatures seem to be everywhere. It's very odd,' said Willbury.

'What do you think is going on?' Arthur asked. He felt bewildered and rather sad.

'I'm not sure, but I don't like it. Think how unhappy those poor creatures were when they arrived at the shop . . . And as for Madame Froufrou . . . Well! The less said about her the better!' He paused for a moment as he thought. 'This business of the hunt leader and Madame

Froufrou looking like brother and sister is strange. I wonder if all this bother is tied up in some way?'

'Do you think your friend Marjorie might be able to help?' asked Arthur.

'I do hope so,' replied Willbury. 'She might not be able to shed any light on this matter of the miniature creatures, but I suppose we should concentrate on our own problems at the moment. Marjorie knows pretty well everybody who has anything to do with mechanics in the town. I am hoping that she will help us track down your wings.

'Who is Marjorie?' asked Arthur.

'Marjorie was my clerk. Very bright woman. She used to deal with patent claims mostly. She could understand most inventions better than their creators, so when I retired she decided to go into inventing. She has a natural aptitude for it. Anyway, she now knows everybody who has anything to do with machines and the like. Though it is quite a secretive world, if you are trusted like she is, you do get to hear what is going on.'

'So do you suppose she might hear where my wings are?'

'That is what I was hoping, but then we still have to get you back underground.' Willbury looked sad.

'Yes . . . I have been thinking about Grandfather . . .' Arthur's voice trailed off.

Willbury put a hand on Arthur's shoulder to comfort him. 'There have to be other ways to get you back into the Underworld.'

'There are,' said Arthur. 'But I just don't know where!'

Willbury stopped in his tracks. 'There are other routes to the underground? This could be very important. Tell me everything!'

'Well, lots of creatures live underground, and not just under Ratbridge . . . Many of their tunnels are linked up. It might be possible to get down one of the tunnels outside Ratbridge, but I don't know where the other tunnels come out above ground . . . And it might be dangerous.'

'Dangerous?' Willbury sounded surprised.

'Yes. I was always warned to stay away from the outer tunnels. Trotting badgers live in some of them . . . and they can be very, very nasty. Grandfather lost a finger to

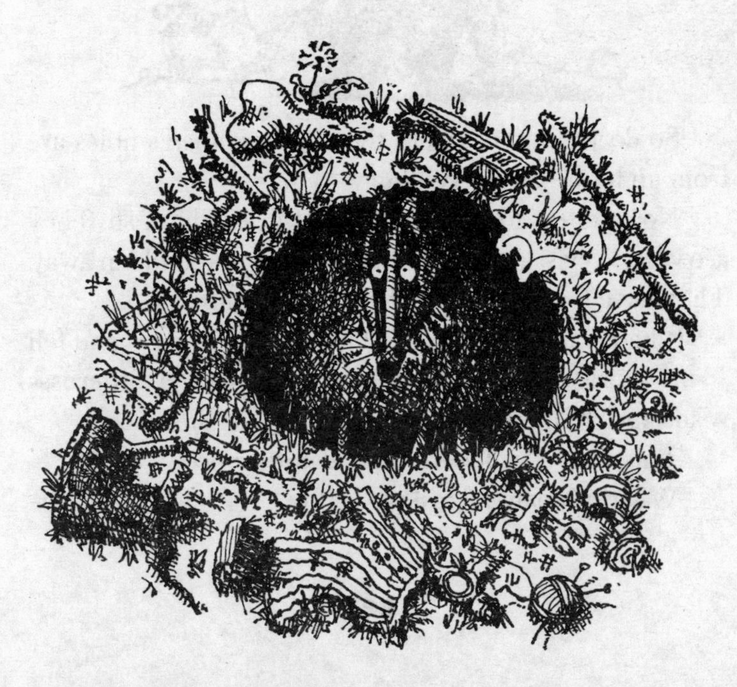

one when he was younger. And there are rabbits . . . and rabbit women too.'

'Rabbit women? I thought they were just a myth.'

'No! They exist. I saw them once when I was exploring . . . well, I didn't meet them . . . but I found a home cave,' replied Arthur.

'Home cave?'

'It's a place where they live. You can tell by the things they leave about—scraps of food, ash, rabbit droppings, and suits the rabbit women have knitted from rabbit wool.'

'So do you know where the rabbit women's holes are from up here?' asked Willbury.

'No.' Arthur looked very sad. 'I don't think so. They are very, very secretive and keep themselves hidden away. They have to . . . to avoid the trotting badgers.'

It had started to drizzle. They both felt glum and fell silent as they walked. Soon they came to a small crossroads and Willbury pointed down one of the streets.

'This way. The Patent Hall is not far now.'

'What is a patent?' asked Arthur.

'Oh! That was my speciality as a lawyer.' Willbury perked up a little. 'A patent is a legal certificate given by the government to the inventor of some new device or idea or process. The patent says that because it is their idea they are the owner of that invention. This gives them the right to use their invention without others copying it without their permission, and the inventor can profit from it.'

'Does that mean that if I had invented string, I could charge everybody who made or sold string?'

'Yes, Arthur, if you had invented string you would be a very, very rich man.' Willbury chuckled.

They turned up another side street and there in front of them stood the Patent Hall. It was a fine building with a frontage that looked like a Greek temple. There was a queue of inventors that started in the street, led up the steps, past the pillared entrance, and disappeared through a huge pair of oak doors. The members of the queue all carried carefully wrapped bundles and looked round nervously at Arthur and Willbury as they passed by.

'Why are they looking at us like that?' asked Arthur.

'They are all worried that someone might steal their ideas before they are registered and patented,' said

Willbury. 'There are people that come here specially to try to steal new ideas, and rob the poor inventors of their patents.'

Willbury led Arthur up the steps of the Patent Hall, and in through the doors. Just inside was a desk where a man was handing out tickets to people in the queue. Beyond was a large crowded hall.

'That is where the inventors give the initial demonstrations. If they get through that they are sent upstairs to have their inventions checked for originality,' said Willbury. 'Now, let us find Marjorie!'

Willbury looked around the hall, walked over to one of the queues, and asked, 'Does anybody know where Marjorie is?' Several arms pointed up to the balcony on the first floor.

Arthur and Willbury set off up the stairs and came to a small tent erected by the side of a desk. Outside it in a deckchair sat a very unhappy looking woman, reading a book of mathematical tables.

'Good morning, Marjorie,' said Willbury. 'I would like you to meet a good friend of mine: Arthur. How are you?'

The woman dropped the book of tables to her lap, then spoke. 'Not well, Mr Nibble. Not well. I have been stuck here for months . . . and things are not looking good!' She paused for a moment, then stood up and reached out a hand to Arthur. 'I am sorry. It is very impolite of me. I am pleased to meet you, Arthur.'

Arthur took her hand, shook it, and gave her a sympathetic smile.

'What's happened?' asked Willbury.

'I came here three months ago with my new invention, did my initial demonstration downstairs, and then was sent up here to see a Mr Edward Trout. He had to check the machine for originality. I was a bit dubious when he said he was taking it away for inspection. Then he didn't come back!'

'What! He disappeared?' asked Willbury.

'Yes! I can prove that I gave him a machine because I've got a receipt, but because it has no description of my machine on it, I can't prove what it is that they have got of mine. They keep trying to get rid of me by sending out junior clerks with any old rubbish they can find in the warehouse! But I won't leave until they give me back my invention!'

'Oh dear, dear me!' said Willbury. 'This is terrible. How have you managed to survive?'

'The other inventors have been very good to me. They have brought me food when they can . . . and this tent and chair. But I can't spend the rest of my life here. What's more, the clerk who disappeared has apparently now left the employment of the patent office, and I am very scared that he ran off with my invention.'

'Ran off with it? What was it?' asked Willbury.

Marjorie looked around furtively, then she whispered to Willbury, 'I know I can trust you Mr Nibble . . . but at this point I think it better that no one knows!'

'Oh!' said Willbury. 'If you are sure. Is it the sort of invention that others might want to steal?'

'Yes! Mr Nibble, it is fantastic,' Marjorie whispered. 'But in the wrong hands it could be very dangerous . . . and now it has either been stolen, or lost!' Marjorie was looking very upset, and Willbury took her hand in his.

'I know it may be of little comfort, but we have brought you some pies from the market,' said Willbury. 'Arthur, could you get them out while I go and have a word with the Head Patent Officer, Mr Louis Trout.'

'Louis Trout?' said Marjorie. 'It was an Edward Trout that went off with my machine.'

'It must be his son – I heard that he joined the office. I am sure Louis will know exactly what has happened.'

'You will never get in to see him, Mr Nibble!' said Marjorie. 'I have been trying for weeks.'

'I think I shall! He knows me from a certain legal case . . . and if I let one or two things drop in conversation with his receptionist I think he will see me very quickly.'

With that Willbury left Arthur and Marjorie, and disappeared into the grandest of the doors along the balcony.

Just five minutes later, there was a noise from the same door. Willbury reappeared looking very flushed and angry.

'What's the matter?' asked Arthur.

'Pack up your things, Marjorie! The Head Patent Officer, Mr Louis Trout, has taken early retirement and gone off to set up a new business with his son . . . the man who disappeared with your invention!'

'They've stolen my machine!'

'I am sorry but it looks as if it might well be that way,' said Willbury. 'There's little point in staying here, though you can file an official complaint . . . Come with us now and I will help you draft one. And besides, I think we need your help. If you come with us I'll explain why.'

They collected up their things and set off back across the town to the shop. Marjorie was muttering about what she might do if she ever caught up with the Trouts, Arthur was worrying about Grandfather, and his wings, and Willbury had a face like thunder.

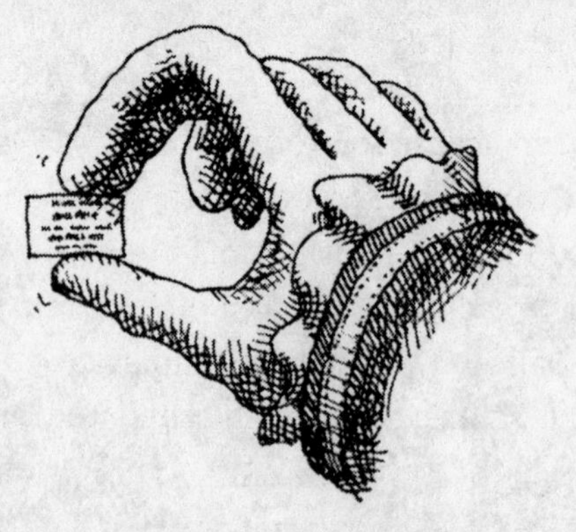

Chapter 11
Gone!

Things took got much worse when they got home. Willbury, Arthur, and Marjorie stood in the doorway of the shop and stared. The door had been broken from its hinges, and inside the comfortable untidiness had been reduced to a broken shambles.

'Oh no!' Willbury whispered under his breath. 'What's happened?'

The room was a pitiful sight. The bookcases were overturned, the curtains torn, and newspapers and books were scattered over the floor. Even Willbury's armchair had been broken and upended.

Willbury cleared his throat then called out. 'Fish! Titus! Egg! Shoe! Where are you?' He was met with silence. 'Where are the creatures?'

Arthur ran across the room to look behind the counter, then out through the door to the back room and hall. He returned looking very glum. 'They're not here.'

Willbury reached down and picked up a torn piece of cardboard, raised it to his nose, and sniffed.

'Fish!' he muttered, and clutched the piece of cardboard to his chest.

Arthur walked towards some newspapers that lay strewn across the floor. Lifting a handful of them, he suddenly let out a gasp. There, huddled on the floor, shaking uncontrollably, was the miniature boxtroll.

'It's Match!' cried Arthur.

The tiny boxtroll ran straight at Arthur and threw its arms around his ankle. Something shiny on the carpet caught Arthur's eye: Match's nut and bolt. Arthur reached down and gently picked up Match, then with his other hand picked up the nut and bolt and passed it to Match's outstretched arms. Match took the nut and bolt and snuggled into Arthur.

Marjorie did not say a word but looked very uneasy as she took in the miniature boxtroll.

'What is it, Marjorie?' asked Willbury.

'Where did these tiny creatures come from?'

'I bought them this morning from an awful man called Gristle . . . ' Willbury stopped. 'He wanted to buy Fish . . . and the other big creatures. I wonder if he was behind this? If so, he is going to pay for it!'

'Willbury, do you think that Gristle has something to do with Madame Froufrou and the creatures at the market?' Arthur asked.

'I am not sure, but whatever is going on, we have got to get Fish and the others back!' declared Willbury. 'I can't help feeling they're in terrible danger.' His eyes fixed on the barrel in the corner. 'Titus!' he exclaimed and rushed to the barrel. Willbury got down on his knees and peered through the hole in the side.

'Oh dear, you poor thing!' said Willbury. He reached inside and pulled the tiny cabbagehead out. 'Titus may be gone . . . but his little friend is still with us.'

Willbury held the miniature cabbagehead in his hand and gently stroked it. It too was shaking.

As Willbury, Arthur, and Marjorie fussed over the tiny cabbagehead, there was a sudden coughing from the shop doorway. They spun round, fearful of who they would see there. But the sight that greeted them was

quite unexpected—a large basket full of dirty washing supported by a pair of legs.

'Good morning! Need any washing done?' The washing lowered itself to the floor, and from behind it stepped a smiling man with a platform made of sticks fixed to his head. On the platform sat a large and friendly-looking rat, wearing a spotted handkerchief tied around his head.

'This is Kipper,' the rat said, indicating the man below, 'and my name is Tom.'

The man pulled out a tiny business card from his pocket, passed it to the rat, who then held it out. Willbury took the card and read it.

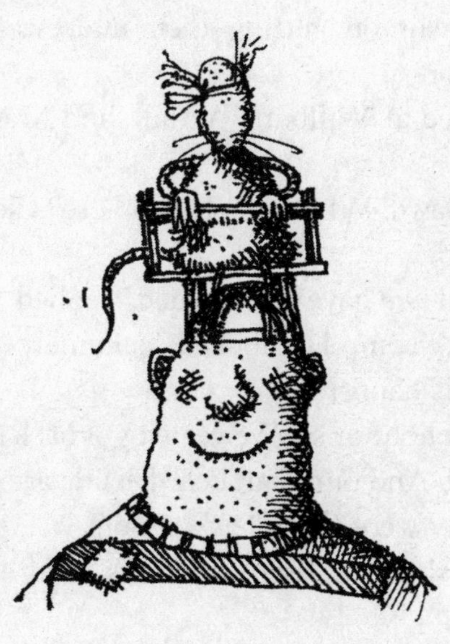

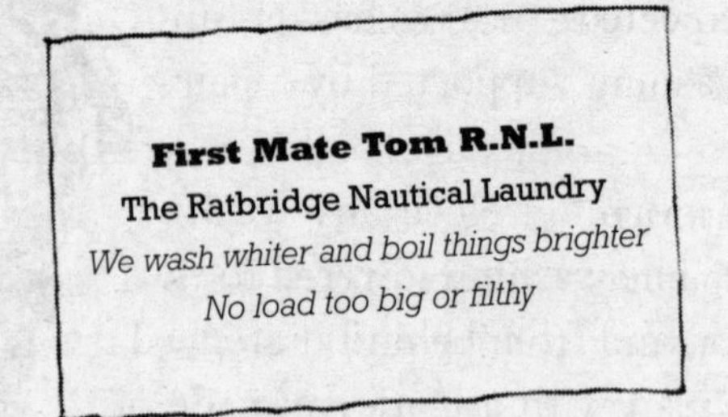

'Now, may we be of any service to you?' said Tom the rat. 'You are very lucky as this week is our "Big Smalls Promotion". As we are new in this area, the Ratbridge Nautical Laundry is offering a special introductory offer to new customers. As much underwear as you like boil washed, free . . . if you get two shirts and a pair of trousers . . .'

Tom stopped. Kipper had just poked him in the ribs.

'I think our friends here have got more on their minds than cheap deals on getting their underwear washed,' said Kipper.

Tom looked at Willbury, Arthur, and Marjorie, then at the shop.

'Oh, my Gawd! What's happened here? Closing down sale?' he asked.

'No, I think we have been raided,' replied Willbury.

'Oh!' said Tom. He looked genuinely concerned. 'When did this happen?'

'In the last hour or so. We've just got back from town,' said Willbury. 'And our dear, dear friends are missing.'

'How many were there?' asked Tom.

'Four—Fish, Shoe, Egg, and Titus,' said Arthur.

'They're three boxtrolls . . . and a cabbagehead,' added Willbury.

'Boxtrolls and cabbageheads?' asked Tom. 'What, like those creatures?'

Tom pointed to Match, who Arthur was still holding, and to the tiny cabbagehead that Willbury was trying to comfort.

'Yes,' said Willbury. 'Only much, much bigger.'

'Oh dear!' said Tom. 'How terrible!'

Then Kipper spoke. 'We've had three of our crew disappear in the last couple of weeks . . . '

'What?' cried Willbury. 'This has happened to you as well?'

'Yes. When the first one disappeared we thought he might have just run away, and he was a nasty piece of work so nobody was sorry to see him go. But last week two more disappeared, Pickles and Levi. They were good mates . . . not the type to run off,' said Kipper. 'Disappeared on a shopping trip.'

'This is very peculiar!' said Willbury. 'Have you got any idea where they might have gone?'

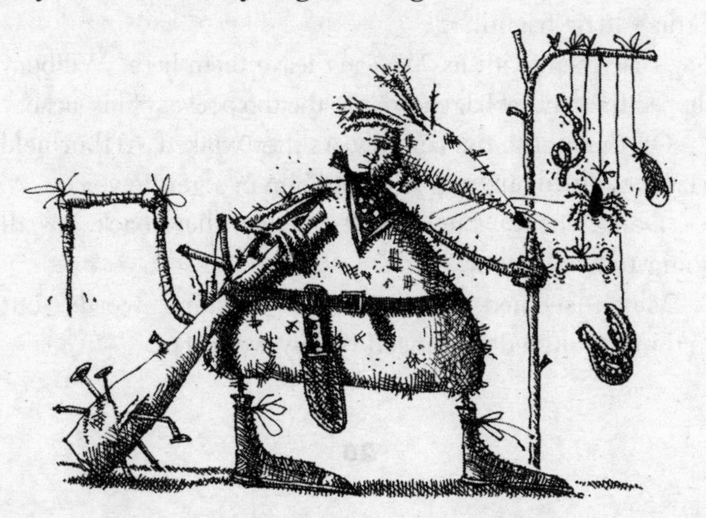

'I think you should talk to the captain,' said Tom. 'He's started an investigation. Why don't you come back with us to the ship?'

Kipper looked up at Tom, and Tom corrected himself. 'Erm . . . laundry?'

'Well . . . ' Willbury looked around the shop. 'I hate to leave the shop like this. But if you think your captain might be able to help us get our friends back, then that's more important.'

'Don't worry about clearing this place up. We can send a party from the laundry to tidy up for you,' said Kipper.

'That is very kind of you, but . . . ' said Willbury.

'Not at all. We insist!' replied Kipper. 'The crew really enjoy tidying things up and cleaning. It's all those years at sea.'

'Well, thank you,' said Willbury.

'Follow us,' said Tom. 'Up Kipper and home! And don't spare the horses!'

Kipper took up the huge laundry basket and pulled its straps over his shoulders.

Arthur turned to Willbury. 'What about Match and Titus's little friend?'

'Take them with us. We can't leave them here.' Willbury slipped the tiny cabbagehead into the top pocket of his jacket.

Off they set to the laundry. As they walked, Arthur held Match tight to him and talked to him in a gentle voice.

'Don't worry, Match, we'll get the others back. It's all going to be all right.'

Match seemed comforted by Arthur's words, but Arthur wondered to himself if they were true.

Chapter 12

Pants Ahoy!

The canal ran along the backs of factories. Once it had been Ratbridge's main commercial link with the outer world, bustling with life. Barges had brought coal and other raw materials to the town, and had taken goods manufactured there out to the world. But since the coming of the steam railway, it had not been much used.

Rain was just starting to fall as the little group led by Kipper and Tom turned onto the towpath. Ahead of them was a very peculiar sight. The aft of a wooden sailing ship filled the canal. Steam rose from a tall chimney positioned on the main deck, and wafted through what looked like ragged sails that were fluttering from the rigging. As they drew closer they could hear a rhythmical hissing and throbbing of machinery. Arthur felt Match twitching.

'What is it, Match?' The miniature boxtroll pointed towards the steam and squeaked.

There was something large and green moving slowly up and down amongst the steam.

'You've got a beam engine!' exclaimed Marjorie.

Kipper turned back and smiled. 'Yes. It's a really big one!'

'Where did you get it from?' Marjorie sounded excited.

Kipper looked a little nervous, and Tom spoke. 'Er . . . We acquired it . . . on a recent trip to Cornwall . . . '

'How do you acquire a beam engine?' asked Marjorie.

'With a great deal of pushing and shoving . . . ' replied Kipper.

'Can't say much, but it was superfluous to the needs of its owners,' said Tom, looking a bit shifty.

'And we won't be going back there on holiday any time soon,' Kipper added.

Willbury gave them a rather suspicious look.

'What's a beam engine?' Arthur asked.

'It's a sort of steam engine, but it usually stays fixed in one place. Instead of moving things like a railway engine, it uses its power to work machines,' Marjorie explained. 'It's a most incredible invention.'

They were approaching the gangplank that ran from the towpath onto the deck of the ship. Arthur looked up and realized the 'sails' were in fact hundreds of pieces of washing, pegged onto the rigging and flapping in the breeze.

'All aboard!' cried Kipper, and the little group made their way up onto the deck of the Ratbridge Nautical

Laundry. Sitting on the rails that ran down both sides of the deck sat some twenty miserable-looking crows.

'What's up, Mildred?' asked Tom.

'Rain!' answered one of the crows. 'We just got this load hung out when it started.'

'Aren't you going to take it in?' asked Tom.

'Doesn't seem much point as it is already wet,' said Mildred. 'Besides, where are we going to put it? The hold is full of dirty washing, the bilges have got another load in, and the crew quarters are packed with boxes of washing powder.'

Tom turned to Willbury, Arthur, and Marjorie. 'I'll take you down below to try and find the captain, but first we need to check in this washing. Kipper . . . the hatch!'

Kipper put the basket down next to a large hatch set in the deck. Then he stamped three times and the hatch opened. A friendly looking rat jumped out.

'Morning, Kipper! Morning, Tom! Got the list to go with this lot?' he asked.

Kipper produced a long strip of paper, and handed it to the rat.

'Can you be very careful with the big woolly underpants, Jim?' said Tom. 'The lady who the pants belong to can only just get them on as it is.'

Jim saluted. 'Aye, aye. Me and the boys will take it from here!' Then he called down the hatch. 'Oi! Lads! Another load . . . and keep an eye on the big pants!'

Suddenly ten more rats jumped out of the hatch, and manoeuvred the basket full of washing down through the hole. The hatch door closed.

'Have you seen the captain?' Tom asked Jim.

'Yes—in his cabin sorting out the lists and invoices. Follow me!' Jim turned and walked aft towards another hatch. The others followed.

'Who were those birds?' Arthur asked Tom as they made their way down some steps inside the hatch.

'Oh, the crows deal with drying and folding. They are part of the crew. What happens is that some of us go out into the town and collect the clothes in baskets. We write it all down on a list so we know who everything belongs to. Then we take it all back to the ship. Jim here then collects the lists, and the rats on the ship divide the washing into different colour and fabric loads. Then the bilge crew put the loads into the bilges and we pump water in from the canal. We add soap powder, and about half a barrel of peppermint toothpaste and then stoke up the beam engine. When the wash is finished, the bilge crew pass the washing up on deck and the crows hang it up to dry. When it's dry, the crows fold it and the rats pack it in baskets to be delivered back to its owners.'

The party had reached the bottom of the stairs and were making their way along a narrow passageway. Jim pointed to a series of pictures that hung on the walls.

'These are the portraits of our captains.'

'There are rather a lot of them,' replied Arthur.

'Yes. We elect a new one every Friday,' said Tom. 'We are very democratic. There is a long tradition of pirates . . . er . . . ' Tom stopped mid sentence, and corrected himself, ' . . . *laundries* electing their own captain.'

They reached the end of the passage and Jim knocked on the door.

'Come in!' came a cry. Jim opened the door and there, behind a huge desk covered in charts and laundry slips, sat a rat with a huge hat on.

'Here's the latest list for you, captain,' Jim said. 'And these are some visitors that Tom and Kipper have brought back.'

'Aye! Aye!' said the captain, as he surveyed the group. 'Who do we have here? Not a complaint about washing, I hope?'

'No, captain, these good people,' said Tom, pointing at Arthur, Willbury, and Marjorie, 'have had a spot of bother. Some friends of theirs have disappeared.'

'Oh dear! We have got something in common then,' said the captain, sounding concerned.

'We may have indeed,' said Willbury. 'May I introduce myself and my friends here. I am Willbury Nibble, and these are my friends Arthur and Marjorie.'

Match gave a squeak. Willbury had forgotten to introduce the tiny creatures.

'Oh, I am very sorry. And this is Match . . . and er . . . a cabbagehead friend in my top pocket here.'

'Good to meet you all,' said the captain, doffing his hat. He looked curiously at the miniature creatures for a moment, then asked, 'How many friends have you lost?'

'Four. Some boxtrolls and a cabbagehead,' answered Willbury. 'They disappeared . . . or were rather snatched . . . while we were at the market.'

'How sure are you that they have been snatched?'

'I am very sure. When we got back to the shop where they lived with me, the place was wrecked. It looked as if there had been a struggle,' answered Willbury.

'When our "colleague" Framley disappeared there were no real signs of a struggle. But it was hard to tell, as his corner of the crew's quarters was always such a mess. He was a right lazy critter . . . and unpleasant

with it,' replied the captain. 'It's only his expertise in the sorting of laundry that we really miss!'

'Tom mentioned that a couple of other rats have gone missing?' said Willbury.

'Yes—Levi and Pickles. About a week later they went shopping in the town and never came back. We miss them . . . Pickles is my brother,' the captain said fondly. 'We sent out search parties, but there was no sign of them.'

'Do you have any clues as to who might have got them?' asked Willbury.

'This is what I have been investigating. There was an incident a few weeks back. We had a visit from a rather odious man by the name of Mr Archibald Snatcher, and a couple of his sidekicks. He said he wanted to welcome us to Ratbridge on behalf of the "New Cheese Guild" and asked if the crew would like to join his guild. Only he was not interested in us rats joining the guild, only the humans! He was really rather unpleasant about rats. Said we couldn't be trusted in the presence of cheese and that we were vermin.

Awful he was! So we showed him and his friends a long walk off a short plank . . . and they took a dip in the canal.'

Kipper and the rats all giggled, but stopped when the captain raised a hand.

'There was something else that happened. That morning, Framley had been picking on the smaller rats, and just as Snatcher arrived, a fight broke out between Jim here, and Framley.'

'I was trying to stop Framley bullying some of the clothes sorters. He turned on me,' said a rather distressed Jim, 'and went for my throat. If Kipper here had not pulled him off, I don't know what he would've done.'

'Anyway it all blew over, what with the visit from strangers and things. But Snatcher had been watching Framley fighting, and afterwards said something to him. Afterwards I asked Framley what it was, and he said that Snatcher offered him a job,' replied the captain.

'It does seem strange,' said Willbury.

'Yes, it does,' said the captain. 'But if he was interested in Framley, how come Levi and Pickles disappeared as well? They were perfectly happy here.'

'What did Snatcher say about this guild of his?' asked Arthur.

'Not very much. Just that it was some sort of mutual organization for the benefit of its members . . . and he kept making jokes about it having "big" plans for Ratbridge,' said the captain.

'What did this Snatcher look like?' Willbury asked.

'Big bloke with sideburns . . . and a glass eye,' replied Jim.

Arthur looked at Willbury. 'It's him! The leader of the hunt . . .'

'Yes,' replied Willbury. 'I think we know who has got your wings . . . and our friends!'

An air of unease filled the cabin.

'I have been investigating where this Snatcher hangs out,' the captain continued. 'He mentioned a building called the Cheese Hall. He said he wanted to restore it to its former glory.'

'I was there last night on the roof,' said Arthur. 'I thought I heard something inside!'

'Interesting,' said the captain. 'I had someone go down and have a look at that place. I'll get him to come and tell you everything he told me.' The captain turned to Jim. 'Do you think you could go and find Bert?'

Jim disappeared out of the door to the cabin.

'Have you contacted the police?' Willbury said.

There was a silence in the cabin, while the crew of the nautical laundry looked awkward.

'I see' said Willbury. 'Does this have something to do with your beam engine?'

'Er . . . Yes . . . and a few other things. We have a

strange relationship with the police,' the captain replied, while avoiding Willbury's gaze.

There was a noise from the corridor. Jim had returned with Bert.

'Ah! Bert,' the captain said. 'Please fill my new friends in on what you told me about the Cheese Hall.'

'Certainly, Guv!' Bert pulled a small notebook out from under his beret. 'Three weeks ago tonight—the second of September at nine thirty-three p.m.—I approached the Cheese Hall from the southern side. The place was boarded up, supposed to be up for sale . . . but I saw lights, and heard things!'

'What things?' asked Willbury.

'Strange, bleating, moaning things!' Bert replied dramatically.

'I heard something like that when I was there,' said Arthur. 'I thought it could have been cheeses.'

'Did you manage to have a look inside?' asked Willbury.

'No. There was no way I could get in—it's mouse and rat proof . . . I asked the local mice. Guess a Cheese Guild would want to keep their cheese safe!' Bert looked thoughtful for a moment. 'Wait. There is one other way in. The mice told me about it. On the roof there's a pair of doors, with a crane that sticks out just above them. It's like one of them Dutch ones they use for lifting pianos into attics and the like. But I don't think there

is any way we can use that, as it's controlled from inside the building.'

One of the other rats raised his hand. 'S'cuse me, but ain't they got a sewer?'

'The mice say the Cheese Hall has got its own cesspit and well. They're not connected up to the main systems, so it's impossible to use those to get in. The place is like a fortress!' said Bert.

'We should storm the place!' said Kipper.

Willbury looked a little shocked. 'We might find ourselves in even worse trouble if we did that . . . But I think we should at least go and have a look.'

'Can we go now?' said Arthur. 'We have got no idea what they might be doing to our friends.'

'I agree,' said Willbury. 'But if they are up to no good in the Cheese Hall it might be as well not to raise their suspicions. I think I should go alone and see what I can find out.'

'I don't like that idea,' said the captain. 'Anything could happen to you. We should all go together. We can observe the Cheese Hall from the Nag's Head Inn opposite.'

'I think we should get the whole crew together for this,' said Kipper.

Willbury turned to his friends. 'I think it best if we leave Match and the cabbagehead here on the ship. They could easily get hurt if there was any trouble.' He turned to the captain. 'Do you have somewhere they could safely stay?'

The captain thought for a moment. 'We have a rather plush box that used to house the sextant before Kipper dropped it over the side. They could use that.'

Kipper was going red, and looked as if he was about to cry. 'Don't worry, Kipper. Nobody knew how to use it anyway.' The captain got down off his chair and pulled a pile of papers off a mahogany box on the floor. Then he opened it. It was lined with deep red padded velvet.

'It's a bit too small for a rat to sleep in but I am sure it would suit your friends here.'

Willbury lifted the tiny cabbagehead out of his pocket from where it had been watching the proceedings and placed it gently in the padded box. It immediately lay down and closed its eyes. Then Arthur leant down and allowed the boxtroll to join the cabbagehead. Match looked round the box and noticed a number of small spare parts fixed to the inside of the lid. He smiled, put his nut and bolt in one corner of the box, then set about quickly removing all the spare parts and piling them up with his nut and bolt. Then he cuddled up to the pile and closed his eyes.

'Thank you. I am sure they will be very happy now,' said Willbury. 'I think we can be on our way.'

After a few minutes' organization, the entire crew of the Ratbridge Nautical Laundry, accompanied by Willbury, Arthur, and Marjorie, set off for the pub.

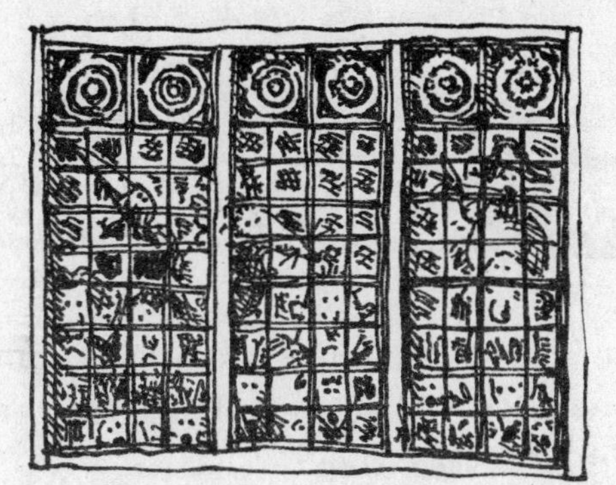

Chapter 13

The Cheese Hall

The group pressed their faces up against the window of the pub, watching the Cheese Hall through the rain. Wooden boards were nailed over most of the windows. It didn't look a very welcoming place.

'I can't see how we're going to get in,' Willbury admitted.

'Storm them with grappling hooks!' said a very enthusiastic Bert.

'We ain't got no grappling hooks, and anyway it looks a pretty tough building to storm,' Tom replied.

'Well, we could go back to the ship and get the cannon?' said Kipper.

'I don't think that the police are going to put up with members of the local laundry letting off cannons in the street,' said Willbury.

'And we ain't got no gunpowder,' said Jim regretfully.'Well, how are we going to find out whether they got our mates then?' asked Tom.

'How about we kidnap one of them and torture 'im!' said Jim.

'Yeah!' agreed Bert.

'I don't think that's quite the right thing to do,' said Willbury. 'I think we have no choice but to watch the place and see what happens. An opportunity may present itself.'

'Does that mean we all get to stay in the pub?' said Kipper hopefully. Tom shot him another disapproving look.

'We just need someone here where they can see the entrance. How about we rent a room and set up watch?' said Arthur.

'Sounds like a very good idea to me,' said Willbury.

'And cheaper than keeping the whole crew in the pub,' added the captain.

'We could keep in touch by using crows as messengers. They could fly back and forth to the laundry,' said Tom.

'I would like to volunteer to act as messenger,' said Mildred as she fluttered and made her way to the front.

'Thank you,' said Willbury. 'And who would like to take first watch?'

'I will,' said Arthur.

'I don't think so,' replied Willbury.

'It's not going to be dangerous just looking out of a window,' pleaded Arthur. 'And besides, it was my idea. I know I can do this, please let me.'

'All right then, but you are only to watch. I think it best though that someone else stays with you,' said Willbury.

Kipper broke in. 'Let me and Tom look after Arthur! We won't let him get into trouble.'

'All right. But if anything happens send a message back to the laundry right away,' insisted Willbury. 'I want to go back with the rest of the crew to check that the little creatures are all right.'

'Me too,' said Marjorie. 'The poor little things seemed so frightened . . .'

Willbury walked over to the bar.

'Excuse me, do you have a room I can rent?' he asked the landlady.

'I am afraid we only have a small one in the attic left,' she answered.

'Does it have a window on the street?' asked Willbury.

'Yes. Who's it for?' she asked.

Willbury pointed out Arthur, Tom, Kipper, and Mildred. The landlady looked rather unsure. 'The crow will have to perch on the curtain rail and it will be extra if boots are worn in bed.'

'Certainly,' said Willbury, and he handed over the money.

The landlady showed Arthur, Tom, Kipper, and Mildred to the room, while Willbury, Marjorie, and the rest of the crew returned to the Nautical Laundry.

Chapter 14

An Incident Outside the Nag's Head

Arthur, Tom, Kipper, and Mildred returned downstairs to the bar and ordered some food. Then they settled at a table in the window of the bar. The rainfell, and slowly it grew dark outside.

By ten o'clock they retired to the attic, having finished fourteen games of Old Maid, twenty-seven games of dominoes, and built a large castle from the crusts of toasted sandwiches.

'Shall I light a candle?' asked Arthur.

'No,' said Tom. 'Best not to. But why don't you open the window, then we will be able to hear if anything is happening.'

Arthur opened the window and looked down. The street was deserted. Tom and Kipper took one of the two single beds and lay down. Mildred perched on the curtain pole and went to sleep. Arthur stood by the window watching. Soon all he could hear was the rain, and Kipper snoring.

Arthur took out his doll, and quietly wound it up.

When it was ready, Arthur whispered, 'Grandfather. It's Arthur! Are you still awake?'

A sleepy voice broke through the crackling. 'Yes, Arthur.'

'How are you?' Arthur asked.

'I could be better,' came the reply. 'It is getting very damp down here. The boxtrolls don't seem to be keeping up with the maintenance. It's playing havoc with my rheumatism.'

'You stay in bed and keep warm.'

'What about you, Arthur? What's happening up there?'

Arthur told him everything that had happened. When he had finished his grandfather remained silent.

'Grandfather . . . Grandfather . . . Are you still there?' Arthur called.

'Listen to me, Arthur,' his grandfather said, no longer a trace of sleepiness in his voice. 'I don't want you to do anything but watch. Mr Archibald Snatcher is a very dangerous man!'

'You know him?' asked Arthur.

'Oh yes . . . I know him . . . ' Grandfather's voice sounded angry. 'And he is the reason we live down here!'

'What!' Arthur was shocked.

'Trust me, Arthur. Stay well away from that man.'

'But what did he . . . ' Arthur broke off as he heard a noise from the street below. 'Sorry, Grandfather . . . but something is happening.' Arthur peered out of the window. Below in the street a shaft of light fell from the open door of the Cheese Hall. Slowly a procession of horses and riders were making their way out into the street. It was the hunt.

'I've got to go, Grandfather.'

'Arthur! Arthur! Be careful!' Grandfather called.

'I will be. Don't worry. I'll talk to you later.'

The doll fell silent, and Arthur tucked it under his suit. Then he shook Kipper and Tom awake.

'Quick! It's the cheese hunt. They're coming out of the hall!' he whispered. 'But I can't see Snatcher!'

Tom scrabbled up onto the windowsill and looked out. There was a yapping and howling as the hounds appeared. A mild panic broke out amongst the 'horses', as they did their best to avoid the hounds.

'Do you think we should send a message to the laundry?' asked Arthur.

'Yes, but let's just wait a few minutes to see what happens,' said Tom. 'Then we might be able to send more useful information.'

A large figure appeared from the door of the Cheese Hall, and the noise in the street subsided. It was Snatcher.

As Snatcher mounted one of the 'horses', the hunt crowded around him. He started talking to his men, but Arthur, Tom, and Kipper could not make out his words.

'Let's get downstairs,' said Tom. 'Kipper, wake up Mildred.'

Kipper reached up and poked the crow. There was a fluttering, and Mildred settled on his shoulder.

Arthur led the way downstairs. He lifted the latch very slowly and opened the front door a few inches, careful not to make a sound. They could hear Snatcher addressing the group.

'The Great One is growing ever greater, and his needs must be met. We must get all the cheese we can tonight. I don't want no slacking. Anybody I catch not pulling their weight . . . ' he paused ' . . . may find themselves in "reduced circumstances" . . . Get my drift?'

'How much longer is we going to have to go hunting for the Great One?' came a voice.

'The time is very near! Soon we will free the Great One, and revenge will be ours!'

Evil chuckling filled the street. A shiver ran down Arthur's spine. What were these men plotting?

Snatcher raised a hand. 'Quiet, my boys! 'Tis time to wend our way.' Snatcher kicked his horse and led off down the street. The hunt followed.

'Quick!' said Arthur. 'Let's follow them!'

'OK. Mildred, can you go back to the laundry and tell them about the hunt?' asked Tom.

Arthur, Tom, Kipper, and Mildred slipped out of the Nag's Head. There was a quiet flapping as Mildred disappeared. Under the cover of the shadows they began to follow the hunt down the street. Suddenly there was a shout.

'Hunt! Whoa! I've forgot me hornswoggle!' It was Snatcher.

'Quick!' said Tom. 'Hide before he comes back.'

Kipper pointed back towards an alley. They turned, ran past the Cheese Hall, and into the alley.

Soon they could hear a 'horse' coming up the street.

Arthur sneaked a look. Snatcher dismounted, unlocked the door of the Cheese Hall and disappeared inside.

'Tom!' Arthur whispered. 'Can you distract the horse? I am going to see if I can get inside the Cheese Hall.'

Tom looked worried. 'It's not safe, Arthur!'

'I know. But it may be our only chance to get our friends back,' replied Arthur.

'I don't think we should let you go in there,' Kipper said.

'Come on! There's no time to argue. I have to do this,' replied Arthur.

Tom and Kipper looked at each other for a moment, and then Tom nodded. He scuttled silently towards the 'horse', and made a very convincing bark. The 'horse' started, then Tom jumped as high as he could and bit one of the 'legs'.

'AAAAAAAH! Blinkin' hound!' came a shout from the horse, and it made off down the street.

Tom waved to Arthur, who ran across to the open door of the Cheese Hall. He looked into the doorway and down the passage. No one was there, but he could hear footsteps.

He rushed in, but Snatcher was turning into the passage. Looking around desperately, Arthur's eye fell on a very large grandfather clock, just inside the door. Arthur opened its case, jumped inside, and pulled the door to. As he pushed against the pendulum and chains, the clock made a loud clang. Snatcher stopped in front of the clock.

'That's odd. It ain't been working for years.' He gave the clock a blow with his hornswoggle, made his way through the front door, and slammed it shut.

Chapter 15

Inside the Cheese Hall

In the passage all was quiet. Then the clock started striking, and as it did, there came muffled squeaking. The chimes died away and the case slowly opened. A very startled Arthur stepped out. He shook his head and blinked, then crept along to the end of the passage. Through an archway was a large entrance hall.

Arthur listened. All was silent and the place was deserted. It seemed as if all the Members of the New Cheese Guild had gone out hunting, but some of them might have stayed behind—he would have to be as careful as he knew how.

He looked about. There was a large marble staircase, several doors, and high up on the walls were statues set in alcoves. These he took to be of heroes of the cheese world. Most of them looked very miserable, apart from one who clutched a flaming cheese aloft and had a mad grin on his face. Arthur walked over to a sign on the wall below this statue and read:

Malcolm of Barnsley
1618–1649
'He lives who has seen cheese combust by its own will'
Donated by the Lactose Paranormal Research Council

Arthur wondered what this meant. Looking around he noticed that the doors all had small plaques fixed to them.

He walked to the closest door and read:

The Members' Tea and Cake Room.
Ladies' Night—February 29th 5.30–6.00p.m.
Non-members keep out!

Arthur he decided to read the plaques on all the other doors as well. On the second it read—

The Chairman's Suite
Entrance by invitation only

At the third . . .

Laboratory

And at the last . . .

KEEP OUT!

I wonder? Arthur thought, and he reached for the handle, turned it, and pushed. The door creaked open to reveal a long torch-lit passageway. Arthur listened. From further down he could just make out a soft bubbling sound. He waited a minute or two, and then his curiosity got the better of him. He made his way quietly down the passage.

At the end he stopped. Before him was a large hexagonal stone chamber, with an open shaft in the centre of the floor. A large yellow banner hung from a balcony. In the centre of the banner was a picture of a wedge of cheese, and beneath it ran the words 'R.C.G. We Shall Rise Again!' His eyes moved back to the open shaft in the centre of the floor, and he realized this was the source of the bubbling sound. He walked forward, and then recoiled. The smell of cheese was overpowering. Holding his nose, he looked down. The shaft descended into total darkness, and the bubbling was coming from somewhere below.

He still had no idea where Fish and the others were.

Arthur noticed a small wooden door on one side of the chamber, with a sign above it: 'Members' Changing Room'. He tried the door. It was locked.

'Bother! 'I'll have to go back to the hall and try the other doors,' he muttered under his breath.

'I don't think they would keep them in a tea room, or the chairman's suite . . . so that leaves the laboratory.' He tried the lab door. It opened.

Arthur found himself at the top of a flight of steps that led down into a vast hall filled with enormous silent machines. Stained-glass windows high in the walls cast an eerie light over everything. Arthur could hear nothing. He decided to risk making a noise.

'Fish . . . Fish . . . are you in here?' he whispered loudly. His voice reverberated alarmingly around the hall before it died away. There was no reply.

As his eyes became accustomed to the gloom, he noticed a pale red glow in a far corner of the lab. It was an illuminated sign above some door or passage, too far away to read.

Arthur nervously made his way down the steps, and crept along the marble pathways between the machinery. The smell of oil and polished brass filled the air. Arthur studied the various machines and apparatus as he passed them by. He recognized some of the machines from his grandfather's bedroom, but his grandfather's were like toys by comparison. There was a beam engine even larger than the one at the laundry, lathes and enormous drills, milling machines, rows of glass tanks filled with liquid that had metal plates hung in them, a cart with an enormous coil of metal sitting on it, and something very large with canvas sheeting tied over it.

Finally he neared the glowing sign. It hung above an archway. Through the archway was a spiral staircase going downwards. He looked up and read:

Arthur looked back around the hall, listened for a moment, and then braced himself. It looked very dark down those steps and Arthur felt nervous about what he might find there. He swallowed and started down.

Chapter 16

The Dungeon

Arthur reached the bottom step, and stopped. Before him was a corridor with six cells—three on either side. The fronts of five of them were made from iron bars, each with a door set into it. But the last cell on the right-hand side was boarded up. Arthur turned to the first cell and peered inside. Eyes stared back at him from the gloom. He could just make out the shapes of the creatures as they quivered against the back wall.

'Oh, poor things! They're underlings!' he said under his breath.

There was a boxtroll, three cabbageheads, and a rare two-legged lonely stoat. Arthur did not recognize any of them.

'Don't worry,' he whispered through the bars. 'I'll get you out of here if I can!' Then he turned round and peered into the cell opposite. There was just a stack of small

cardboard boxes, so he walked on. As he reached the next cell, a flash of movement came from the darkness, and suddenly snarling heads appeared between the bars and snapped at him. Arthur jumped back. They were trotting badgers.

Arthur watched them till they stopped snapping, quietened down, and finally returned to the gloom at the back of their cell. Then, shakily, he turned to inspect the cell behind him. There were three more boxtrolls. Arthur felt his heart jump, but as soon as he took a better look he realized none of them were his friends. Again he whispered some words of reassurance before moving on to investigate the last iron-barred cell.

Three very familiar cardboard boxes were stacked on top of each other.

'Fish! Shoe! Egg!' Arthur called, then waited for a few moments. Eventually a head rose from a hole in the top box. It was Fish.

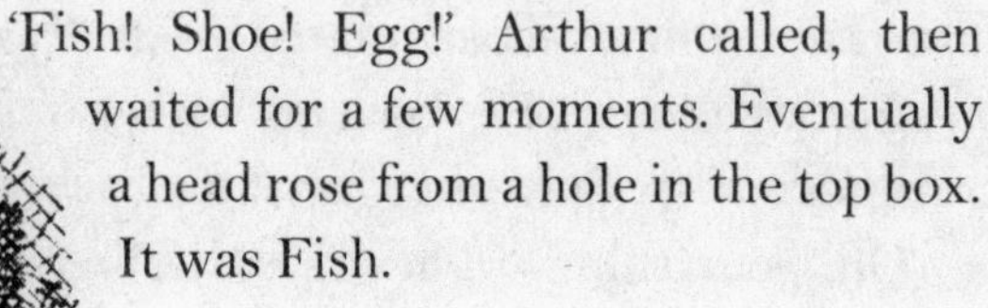

Fish gave a loud gurgle, and heads, arms, and legs sprouted from all three boxes simultaneously. The stack fell over with a clatter and was followed by a lot of moaning. Titus was standing behind where the

stack had once stood. He smiled at Arthur. Arthur clutched the bars as his friends rushed forward to meet him.

'Thank God you are all right!' exclaimed Arthur. 'We have been so worried about you.'

Fish, Shoe, and Egg all gurgled excitedly, while Titus squeaked. They all reached their hands through the bars towards Arthur, and looked at him very hopefully.

'I am going to get you out of here!' Arthur said firmly. 'I promise.' He looked down at the lock.

'I don't suppose you know where the key is, do you?' asked Arthur.

The underlings shook their heads and looked disappointed. Arthur turned round. There was no key visible anywhere, but his eye fixed on the boarded-up cell opposite.

It might be worth taking a look at that.

Arthur was stopped dead in his tracks. Several pairs of hands were gripping his clothes and holding him back.

'All right,' said Arthur to his friends. 'I won't go near it.'

The hands holding his clothes let go. Arthur studied the front of the boarded-up cell. A large switch was fixed to the planks by its door, and underneath it, written in red paint, was:

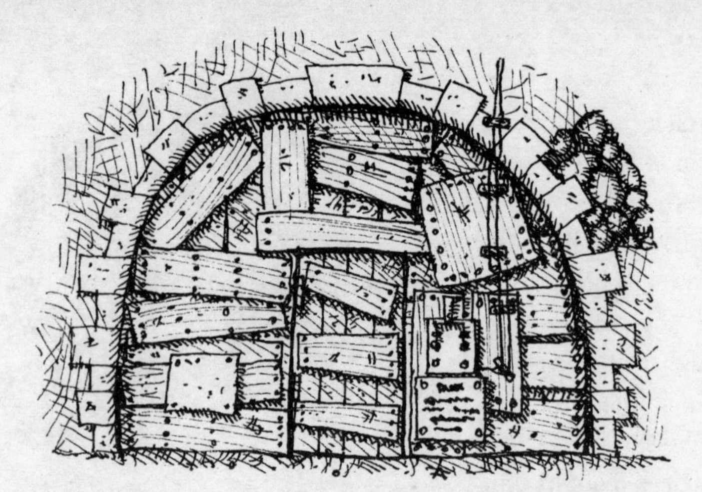

Beware!
Dangerous Prisoner!
Put switch in upright position
BEFORE entering the cell!

'What's in there?' Arthur asked.

The underlings started jumping up and down, and making noises. 'Bonk! Bonk! Bonk!'

When they realized that Arthur had no idea what they meant, they gave up.

'Well, I had better concentrate on getting you out of here anyway!' The underlings looked relieved.

'I think the key must be upstairs somewhere. I'll go and see if I can find it. I will be back soon—I promise!'

Arthur turned and made for the steps, keeping well away from the boarded-up cell and the trotting badgers.

Chapter 17

Back in the Lab

Arthur crept up the stairs from the dungeon. Where would they keep the key? he thought, and he decided to search the lab. As he tiptoed amongst the machines he noticed some chains stretching down from the darkness to somewhere near the centre of the lab. After a while Arthur emerged from between machines, and found he was standing on a path-way that surrounded a large open area. Beyond waist-height railings were a huge set of iron doors, set in the floor. The chains that he'd seen were fixed to iron rings in the centre of the doors. High above hung a strange giant metal funnel. Its mouth pointed down towards the doors.

Arthur walked around the pathway. When he reached the far side there was a box fixed to the railings—

some kind of control panel. A metal tube ran down from beneath it, and through a small hole by the edge of the pathway. He peered down the hole. It was dark and very narrow, but he could just make out a pale light from somewhere deep below. Again he caught the strong smell of cheese.

He turned back to the control panel. There was an array of dials, and below them was a brass disc with a slot for a key. The slot was pointing to the word 'DOWN' that had been etched into the front panel. Across the panel was etched the word 'UP'. Arthur looked out across the doors, and then his eye followed the chains up towards the funnel. From the top of the funnel giant curling wires descended to the roof of what looked like an iron garden shed on stilts. This shed stood by the pathway, and overlooked the doors in the floor. Another pair of curly wires emerged from the shed roof, and led to a smaller funnel. This was fixed above the roof of an empty cage that stood on the floor of the lab next to the shed. He had a bad feeling about it.

There were steps leading up to a gantry that ran around the shed. Arthur made his way up them, then looked into the shed through its thick glass windows. A chair stood in front of a large console covered in buttons, levers, and switches. Behind the chair was a workbench scattered with bits and pieces. There was some small machine with two funnels attached to it, some tools, a pile of cogs and springs . . . a wooden box . . . and . . . his wings.

Arthur rushed around to the door, and tried the handle. Locked. He looked in again. They were definitely his wings.

And the wing spars and leatherwork had been mended. Then his heart stopped. They had taken the box to pieces!

'Oh no! What am I going to do now?' he muttered. 'I need to find keys!' Perhaps the keys for the shed and the keys for the cells would all be kept together somewhere.

He looked about the lab. There didn't seem to be anywhere obvious that keys would be kept. Arthur climbed back down the steps, made his way across the lab, and up the steps to the entrance hall.

He crept across the hall to the Chairman's Suite. It wasn't locked, and in a moment he was inside with the door closed.

The room was dark and smelt rather unpleasant. The faces of generations of Snatchers stared down at Arthur from family portraits on the walls making him feel uneasy.

Don't look at them, and you will feel better, Arthur told himself.

He looked about the room. A desk stood at one end, huge and very cluttered, and behind it heavy, moth-eaten velvet drapes covered the wall. In front of a fireplace were two decrepit sofas and a chaise longue. One of the sofas had an old blanket and a dirty sheet strewn over it, and next to it was a pile of dirty socks. The other sofa was a mess of horsehair and springs. Someone had cut its cloth covering away.

The desk seemed the obvious place to look. Arthur noticed an area in the centre of the desk had been cleared so a large sheet of paper could be laid out. This was held down at its corners by a paperweight, a dirty cup and saucer, and a pair of old boots. Arthur studied the sheet. It seemed to be some sort of scientific diagram, but more than that he could not tell.

Around it on the desk were stubs of old pencil, rubber bands, a broken pocket watch, the dried remains of half a sandwich, a ruler, and a broken quill . . . but no keys. Arthur decided to try the drawers. He walked around the desk and pulled open the first one.

It was filled with socks, only a little less grubby than the pile by the sofa. Reluctantly he put his hand in and searched to see if there were any keys hidden there. When he decided there were not, he moved on.

Arthur opened the next drawer, and to his disgust he discovered it contained long johns. There was no way he was putting his hand in there. He took the ruler from the desk and used it to empty the drawer. Again there were no keys, so he put the underwear back, using the ruler. Then he closed the drawer very firmly, dropped the ruler as hastily as he could, and shivered.

With a slight feeling of dread, he opened the next drawer. In this one he found a pink wig. Arthur recognized it immediately—it was the wig Madame Froufrou had been wearing in the market. So there *was* a connection between her and Snatcher. But there was no time to think about that now—he had to concentrate on looking for the keys.

He lifted the wig out of the drawer, gave it a shake, and then hunted around the empty drawer. No keys!

Arthur moved on to the last drawer. This one was so full that it was hard to open, and he had to pull with all his might. When it finally sprang open, he found a great bundle of fabric crammed inside. He pulled it out and opened it up, then gave another gasp of recognition. It was Madame Froufrou's dress.

Things get curiouser and curiouser, Arthur thought. He checked the drawer for keys, and stuffed the dress back into it, though wasn't easy.

Where next? Arthur wondered. Looking about the room, he noticed a small table by one wall. There was a glass bottle on the table with some objects in it. Arthur walked over and picked it up. In the bottom, amongst some straw, was a tiny piece of cheese and two very small sleeping mice . . . or very, very, very, small rats.

As he stood looking at the tiny creatures in puzzlement, a sudden noise came from outside the room. Footsteps—approaching the door. Arthur froze for a second, then ran to the drapes and flung himself desperately behind them. A moment later someone entered the room.

'My poor feet! This blooming rain!' It was Snatcher's voice.

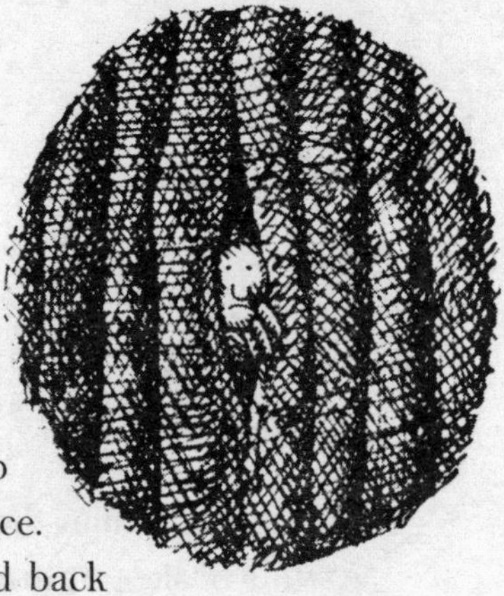

Arthur peeped out from behind the curtains. Snatcher had his feet up on his desk and was unlacing his wet boots. He took them off and swapped them with the dry pair on the desk. Then Snatcher stood up and walked over to the fireplace. He stood by the fire and pulled back his coat. Then Arthur saw them!

Hanging from a short piece of string attached to Snatcher's waistcoat was a large bunch of keys. After a few moments trying to warm himself, Snatcher gave up, turned, and walked out of the door, leaving it slightly ajar.

Arthur crept out from behind the drapes and made his way across the room. He looked out into the hall and saw Snatcher standing in the archway facing the front door.

I have got to get those keys, thought Arthur. But how to do it? Then he heard a commotion from the passage.

'Come on, me lads! How many cheeses did we get in the end?' Snatcher asked someone in the passage.

'Eight, I think!'

With a sinking heart, Arthur realized that the hunt was returning. He needed to find a good hiding place—and quickly.

'Put the mutts in my suite,' Snatcher ordered.

Arthur looked back at the velvet drapes and thought better of it. Then he looked at the staircase. Perhaps he could hide upstairs? He crept out of Snatcher's suite,

made his way to the staircase, and started to climb as fast as he could. Behind him he heard more voices.

'The others made me be legs for the whole hunt!' It was Gristle.

'Stop your complaining, and get upstairs and man the cheese hoist,' Snatcher barked.

Arthur broke out into a cold sweat, and increased his pace up the stairs. As he reached the top he looked back. Gristle was just reaching the first step. Arthur rushed for the only door on the landing. In a second he was through it with the door closed.

He found himself in the roof space below the dome. Fenced pens filled with hay covered most of the floor. At the far end of the loft a pair of doors were open to the night sky—these must be the doors that Bert had described.

He heard Gristle again. 'Oi! Master. Can you send me up some help? I'm knackered.'

Arthur felt sick. He rushed to the open doors and looked down. Far below in the street he could see huntsmen and cheese-hounds milling about.

'Oi! Snatcher! I can't lift these cheeses on me own!'

Arthur looked up. Above his head was a metal beam that protruded out above the street. A pulley with a rope going through it hung from the end of the beam.

The door behind him opened. Arthur held his breath and jumped for the rope.

Chapter 18

Out on the Roof!

He had only just made it. Arthur sat on the bridge of the roof and recovered his breath. It was still raining, and a few inches behind him was a vertical drop to the street. He did not feel happy.

Keeping his eyes straight ahead, Arthur shuffled along the roof until he reached the statues below the dome. He could hear muffled voices.

Then a metallic squeaking started. Arthur looked round. He could just see the pulley at the end of the metal beam. The wheel in the pulley was turning and a rope slowly passed through it.

The plaintive bleating of cheeses grew louder.

'The poor things,' Arthur muttered, then he looked up at the dome. Set into the dome were several small round windows. These, he thought, must act as lights for the loft. He decided to have a look and see what was going on in there.

Arthur made his way along to a narrow strip of stonework that ran around the base of the dome. One of the windows was just a few feet from him. He eased himself along the ledge and peered in. Below he could see that the pens were now occupied by cheeses. He moved around to the far window so he could see what was happening by the hoist.

Several men were pulling something up. After a great deal of rope had been pulled in, a net came into view. More cheeses! When the net was level with the doors, one of the

Members took a long pole with a hook on the end, and used it to pull the net into the loft. Then the doors were shut and the cheeses released from the net. For about a minute there was mayhem as the cheeses did all they could to evade capture. But trapped in the loft the cheeses stood no chance, and soon they were all in pens.

The cheeses quietened down, and the Members disappeared downstairs. Arthur decided it was too dangerous to try and get back down the hoist and, besides, the loft doors were shut. But he had to get back in somehow. He pushed at the little window in front of him and was surprised when it gave way fairly easily, swinging open without too much noise. Arthur peered through it. Directly below him was a pen, with a good covering of hay on the floor. He turned around, lowered himself through the window, and dropped. He hit the floor, just avoiding a cheese, and fell back into the soft hay. The cheeses in the pen started bleating loudly once more. Arthur sat still, hoping their noise would not bring any of the huntsmen

back. But as the bleating died down he heard footsteps coming up the stairs. He groaned inwardly, but quickly covered himself in the hay and lay very still.

'Them cheeses is making a right commotion! You'd think they knew what was going to happen to them!' said a voice—Gristle. 'Let the cage down, and get them out the pens. Snatcher says that the Great One is going to be right hungry after they give him a good zap!'

'What they going to use tonight?' asked another voice.

'Those awful trotting badgers,' replied Gristle. 'Did you see what they did to the Trouts?'

'Yes. Old Trout won't be able to sit down any time soon, and Trout Junior is lucky he still has a nose.'

Arthur peered out through the hay and saw Gristle and two other men standing in the loft. Gristle was beside a pair of brass levers that stuck out of the wall.

'Move yerselves then,' ordered Gristle. 'Don't want to squash yer.'

The other men cleared a space under the centre of the dome, and Gristle pushed one of the levers down. Arthur followed the men's gaze upwards. A cage was descending from inside the very top of the dome. It clanked and shook as it moved slowly towards the floor of the loft. The cheeses were silent. The cage settled on the floor.

'Right!' said Gristle. 'Let's get the cheeses in.'

While one of the men held the cage door open, Gristle and the other man grabbed cheeses from the pens and pushed them in. Soon the cage was full.

'I do hope the Great One is hungry! Eight is an awful lot of cheese,' said the doorman.

'Don't worry, he is getting really BIG!' smirked Gristle.

'Snatcher says he will be ready real soon. All we have to do is keep up the supply of cheese and monsters.'

Arthur felt cold when he heard this. What was going on?

'Oi! Gristle! D'yer think they're ready yet?'

'The music ain't started! They 'ave to 'ave the music before the cheese goes in the pit. Otherwise it wouldn't be a Cheese Ceremony . . . would it?' Gristle replied. 'Just keep your ear out for the din.'

All was silent in the cheese loft until strange music started to waft up from somewhere below. Arthur had never heard anything like it before. It was a crazed drumming and blowing of horns. It reached a crescendo then stopped.

''Ere we go!' Gristle pushed down the second lever. A trapdoor beneath the cage opened with a bang. The cage full of cheeses shuddered. Gristle pushed the first lever down and the cage started to disappear through the hole.

After about thirty seconds Gristle spoke again. 'The chain's gone floppy. It must have hit the fondue!'

'Let it sink slowly, then after about a minute haul it up,' whispered one of the others. 'Don't want no half-cooked cheeses hanging about!'

Gristle waited, then brought the cage back up. It came through the floor . . . empty, just a few strings of molten cheese hanging from the bottom. Gristle stopped the cage, then snapped the trapdoor lever up, and the door in the floor closed.

'Done!' said Gristle. 'Time for tea and biscuits.' The Members trooped out of the loft and closed the door. Arthur knew he had witnessed something awful, but he was not sure quite what.

Chapter 19

Tea and Cake

Arthur opened the door of the loft a few inches. He could hear distant laughing, and the chinking of crockery. He closed it again.

He turned and looked at the cage that stood in the centre of the floor. It was a very sad sight. Arthur climbed back into one of the pens and lay down in the hay to think.

'I've got to get back downstairs to rescue the underlings . . . and what am I going to do about my wings? I'll never be able to put them back together without Grandfather . . . ' Arthur sat up and pulled out his doll. 'Grandfather!'

He wound the doll, and then called his grandfather's name.

'Arthur! Where have you been? Where are you? Are you all right?'

'I am all right, Grandfather . . . but I am in the loft above the Cheese Hall.'

'WHAT? You're in the Cheese Hall?' Grandfather sounded angry.

'Yes . . . ' said Arthur, then he explained what had happened.

'Oh, Arthur! Why can't you do what you're told? I'm very cross with you . . . and Mr Nibble. He should never have let you get into this trouble.'

'It's not his fault. He told me not to take any chances and I disobeyed him . . . and you.'

'Well, we will talk about this later!' Grandfather sounded very serious. 'But for now, we need to get you out of there. If you can find a few tools I can tell you how to put your wings back together, if you can somehow get to them. Then you'll be able to escape!'

Arthur paused before he spoke again. 'I have to help the underlings escape as well.'

'Yes,' said Grandfather, 'but you'll be no use to them if you can't escape yourself. You need to get your wings fixed.'

'But what should I do?' asked Arthur.

'If you hide for a while, I bet the Members will go to sleep before too long. Then get down to the lab and find a way of getting the wings. I'll guide you through rebuilding the motor.'

'All right, Grandfather. And how are you doing?'

'This damp is getting worse and all my joints are aching. About an hour ago I heard some rumbling. It sounds as if some of the caves are starting to crumble. I don't know what those damn boxtrolls think they are playing at. They are supposed to keep this place dry, and shored up.'

Arthur felt worried about Grandfather. 'Are you going to be all right?'

'I'll be fine. Anyway, you get some rest! Contact me as soon as you get hold of your wings.'

'I will, Grandfather . . . and keep warm!'

The crackling from the doll stopped and Arthur lay back in the hay. He tried to concentrate on the noise from downstairs, but soon his eyes closed and he dropped off to sleep.

He awoke with a start. Something long and yellow was pecking his nose. He sat up, and as he did two black shapes flapped up and settled on the edge of the pen.

'Sorry if we startled you.' It was a pair of crows.

'You did!' replied Arthur as he rubbed his nose. 'But I'm pleased to see you!' The crows must have flown in through the window he'd forced open.

'We're from the laundry. The captain and the others are very worried about you.'

'How did you know I was here?' Arthur asked.

'We saw you on top of the dome earlier, and we reported it to the captain, and your friends. They asked us to fly over here to see if we could find you.'

'Can you take a message back to them for me?'

'No problem!' cawed one of the crows.

'Tell them that I've found the underlings in the dungeon under this place . . . and Snatcher and the Members have built some huge weird device . . . And they are doing really nasty things to cheeses . . . Oh! And I have found out where my wings are . . . '

'Is there anything else we can do?' asked the other crow.

Arthur thought for a moment, and then listened. There was no noise from downstairs. 'Yes. Could you fly down the outside of the building and check through the windows to see if Snatcher and his mob are asleep?'

'No sooner said than done!' The crows set off through the open window in the dome. After about a minute they returned.

'It's all clear. We flew round the whole building and looked in every window we could. They're all asleep in a big room at the front. Looks like they've had a right feast of cake. Even that Snatcher is in there, snoring away.'

'Good!' said Arthur. 'Thank you—and tell them we'll all be back soon.'

The crows disappeared and Arthur set off down the stairs.

When he reached the bottom he crept across to the tea room. As quietly as he could he opened the door. About thirty men were strewn across sofas and old armchairs, surrounded by the debris of an enormous feast of tea and cake. On the far side of the room in the largest armchair the sleeping Snatcher was slumped.

A cold sweat broke out on Arthur's forehead. He would have to be very, very careful. Trying not to make the slightest noise he made his way into the room and started to weave his way between the furniture, and the abandoned teacups and plates on the floor. Slowly he got closer. The legs of one of the Members lay across his path and Arthur stepped over them. As he did the hem of his vest brushed the Member's foot.

'CAKE!'

Arthur jumped forward and turned. It was Gristle.

'. . . just one more slice . . . I love cake . . .' Gristle's eyes were still closed. He was talking in his sleep. Arthur closed his eyes for a moment and swallowed, then made the last few steps to Snatcher.

The keyring hung on a string from Snatcher's waistcoat. There was a gentle jingling as Snatcher's enormous belly moved in and out.

On a cake stand that stood on the floor was a knife. Arthur picked it up, and gently took hold of the keys. He held the knife to the string and as Snatcher's belly moved the knife cut slowly into the string. The string separated and for a moment Snatcher's belly wobbled. Arthur held his breath. Snatcher snorted . . . but didn't wake. Arthur held the keys tight, put the knife down and crept out of the room.

Arthur rushed into the lab and to the shed. He made his way up the steps and searching amongst the keys he found one that fitted the door. He slid it in the lock and turned. There was a satisfying clunk. He tried the handle, and the door opened. Arthur reached inside his suit and took out his doll.

'Grandfather! Are you there?'

'Yes, Arthur.'

'I am in the lab with the wings. Can you help me put them back together?'

'Certainly, Arthur. Can you find a small screwdriver and an adjustable spanner?'

Arthur looked about the bench and found the tools he needed. 'Yes! I've found them.'

'Good.'

Over the next hour Grandfather instructed as Arthur rebuilt the wings' motor. Occasionally Arthur looked up to check the door to the entrance hall, or would have to break off to wind up the doll when his grandfather's voice started to fade. Finally the motor was back together.

'I think it would be a good idea if you put the wings on and wound them up . . . just in case,' said Grandfather.

Arthur strapped the wings on. 'You're right. And thank you, Grandfather. I will speak to you later. I've got underlings to rescue before Snatcher wakes up!'

'Very well, Arthur,' said Grandfather. 'But make sure you call me as soon as you are out of there! And please, please try not to take any unnecessary risks.'

Arthur put the doll away and quickly wound up his wings, locked the shed and made his way back downstairs. He peered in at the Members, but they were all still snoring away. Arthur prayed that they would stay asleep for long enough. Tiptoeing on, he headed back towards the dungeon.

Chapter 20

An Escape?

Arthur stopped in his tracks as he entered the dungeon. The door of the trotting badgers' cell stood open. He glanced across to his friends' cell. The four of them were still pressed up against the bars, looking very happy to see him. He silently pointed to the open cell door. Fish shook his head and gave him a thumbs up.

Arthur mouthed the words, 'HAVE THEY GONE?'

Fish nodded his head. Arthur sighed with relief, and made his way to his friends' cell.

'I am going to get you out of here,' Arthur said and produced the keys. He unlocked the door, and the underlings ran out and hugged him. Arthur hugged them back.

'Now,' said Arthur. 'We had better unlock the others.'

Fish pointed to the cells with the other underlings in, and nodded.

'What about the boarded-up cell?'

The underlings looked across at it, and shook their heads.

'Why not?' asked Arthur.

Again they started to jump up and down, and quietly made bonk! bonk! noises.

'I'll trust your judgement,' Arthur said, feeling a little nervous. 'It might be very dangerous to release whatever is in there.' The underlings looked relieved.

Arthur unlocked the other underlings, and soon all of them stood at the bottom of the stairs.

'Come on!' said Arthur. 'We have to get out of here quickly . . . but remember to keep very quiet.'

He guided the underlings up the stairs and out through the lab to the door to the entrance hall. Arthur was about to lead the underlings out into the hall when there was a loud cheese bleat from the passageway to the front door. Arthur and the underlings froze. After a few seconds the door of the tea room opened and a sleepy Gristle walked out.

Snatcher's voice followed him. 'It'll be the milkman. Tell 'im to leave fifteen pints and that I will pay 'im next week.'

Arthur watched as Gristle disappeared down the passage.

Then he heard Gristle shout.

''Ave you got the keys to the front door?'

Arthur felt a lump in his throat. He looked from the archway to the passage across to the tea room.

There was a pause then Snatcher's voice boomed from the tea room. 'Someone's nicked me blooming keys!'

Arthur ushered the underlings forward. 'Up the stairs! Run for your lives!' he whispered.

Just as they started to scuttle across the hall, there was a commotion from the tea room and Snatcher stepped through the door. Arthur looked at Snatcher in horror. This might be the end of everything.

Unable to control the panic in his voice, Arthur turned to the underlings and shouted:

'RUN!'

The underlings rushed up the stairs. Arthur pushed the buttons on the front of the wing box and jumped up. Thank goodness he could fly again.

'It's that blasted boy again. And he's stolen my wings!' shouted Snatcher. The other Members piled out into the entrance hall, looking up at Arthur, then at the underlings fleeing up the stairs.

'Get 'em!' screamed Snatcher, grabbing a walking stick from a coat stand outside the tea room door, and raising it to throw at the underlings. Arthur threw the keys hard at Snatcher. They caught him in the face and Snatcher wailed at Arthur.

'You little swine. Just you wait till I get 'old of you!' But Arthur was already too far off the ground for Snatcher to reach.

Some of the Members had reached the stairs and were gaining on the underlings. Arthur adjusted his wing speed and flew up to one of the alcoves above the Members and grabbed hold of the statue. Then he pulled it hard. The statue toppled over. Below, the Members saw what was happening and ran back down the stairs to get out of the way. The statue crashed down on the stairs.

Snatcher screamed again. 'Don't stop! Get those Monsters!' He grabbed another walking stick and waved it at the Members.

Arthur flew to the next statue and waited till some of the Members were brave enough to start mounting the stairs again, then he pulled on it. Again there was a crash as the statue hit the stairs, and again the Members ran back to avoid it.

The underlings reached the door to the loft, rushed through it and disappeared. Arthur turned off his wings, ran through the door, and slammed it closed as a walking stick clattered against it.

The underlings were standing in the loft looking scared out of their wits. Arthur looked around—they needed to barricade the door. His eyes fixed on the cage. He turned on his wings again, flew to the top of the cage, and unhooked it from its chain.

'Quick! Push this cage against the door,' Arthur shouted to the underlings.

The underlings obeyed and soon the cage crashed against the door. Arthur flew to the doors at the far end of the loft and pulled them open. The net was hanging from the end of the beam.

'Fish. Let out a bit of the rope so I can get the net into the loft!' Arthur ordered. Soon he was spreading the net out on the floor.

'Everybody get in it.' The underlings looked horrified.

'Quick!' shouted Arthur, above crashes as the Members threw themselves against the door. 'This is our only chance!'

Reluctantly the underlings climbed into the net, and Arthur held the rope, then he pulled it in. There was a fearful squeaking and moaning, and the net swung out over the street.

'When you get to the ground, get out of the net and make for the canal,' Arthur called over to the underlings. 'Don't worry about me—I'm going to fly.'

Slowly he paid the rope out and the frightened creatures disappeared.

The crashing at the door grew louder, and Arthur let the rope out faster.

Finally the rope went limp.

'Get them!' screamed a voice. The Members were racing across the loft. But there was just one problem. Before Arthur could fly again, he needed to wind up his wings. He reached for the knob, but at the same moment he felt someone grab at his arms and pull them back. He twisted around. It was Snatcher.

Chapter 21

Back Below the Cheese Hall

Snatcher wasted no time in dragging Arthur back down to the dungeon and instructing Gristle to unstrap his wings. The Members surrounded Arthur.

'What are we going to do with you, my little thief?' asked Snatcher, dangling the wings in front of him.

'I am not the thief!' snapped Arthur.

'Oh, yes, you are! You took my wings!'

'Those were my wings. You stole them from me in the first place.'

'That is as maybe, but they are mine now. And for all the grief you've caused me, I think pretty much everything of yours is as good as mine. Search 'im!'

The Members descended on Arthur, and emptied his pockets.

'Not much here, guv!'

'Wait. He's got something up his jumper!'

'Get it!' ordered Snatcher.

Arthur tried to defend his doll with his cuffed hands, but he was overpowered.

'What have we here?' asked Snatcher. 'The little boy has got a little dolly!'

'Ahhhh!' scoffed the Members.

Snatcher laughed and threw it on the floor. 'By the time I've finished with you, that dolly is going to look like your big brother.'

The Members laughed.

'What do you mean?' asked Arthur.

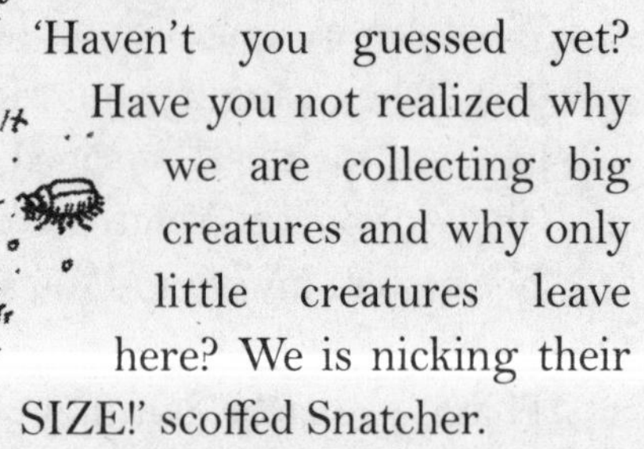

'Haven't you guessed yet? Have you not realized why we are collecting big creatures and why only little creatures leave here? We is nicking their SIZE!' scoffed Snatcher.

Arthur froze. 'Size?'

'Yes!' Snatcher laughed. 'It so happens that we have come by a certain device . . . ' he stopped and winked at the Trouts, who were holding Arthur, ' . . . that can extract the size from things. All your little friends who came our way are now your even littler friends.'

Snatcher and the others now all burst out laughing.

'But what for?' Arthur asked.

'That is for us to know. It is part of our BIG plan.' There was more laughter. Then Snatcher's face changed, and his voice turned nasty. 'But I needed them monsters you freed. Perhaps you might like to donate some of your size instead?'

Arthur did not reply.

'Yes. I thought that might shut you up. Now we have to go and find a load more monsters to shrink!' snarled Snatcher. He turned to the Trouts. 'Throw him in a cell. We'll sort him out the next time we fire up the machine.' Then he smirked horribly. 'And next time I go out on a little selling trip, I am sure all the ladies will be falling over themselves to buy a miniature boy!' He looked directly at Arthur, put on a simpering face and spoke in the unmistakable tones of Madame Froufrou: 'I 'ave only one of zese little creatures, for sale to ze most fashionably rich lady of all!'

Arthur gaped. So that explained why Madame Froufrou had reminded him so strongly of Snatcher! It was just a disguise!

The Trouts lifted Arthur and threw him into the cell that had contained the trotting badgers. Snatcher walked over and locked the door.

'When are we going to fire up the machine . . . ?' asked Gristle.

'The sooner the better,' replied Snatcher. 'But there is no point doing it just for the boy, we need some more monsters to put in it. We need to go down below . . . '

Arthur noticed the Members looking worried at this, ' . . . but first I think a quick cup of tea is in order.' They all set off up the stairs leaving Arthur alone in the dungeon.

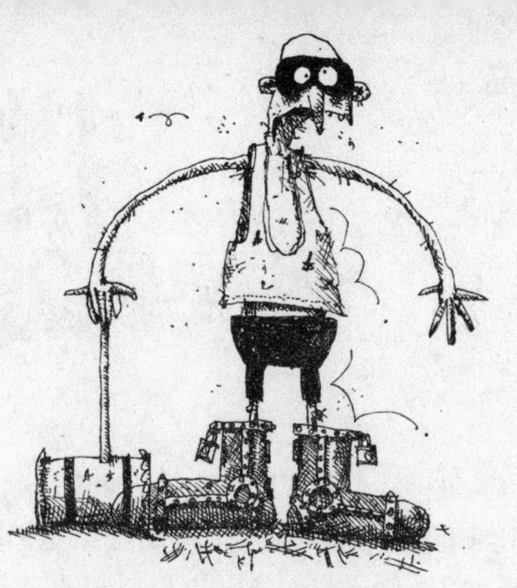

Chapter 22

The Man in the Iron Socks

Alone in the cold dank dungeon, Arthur looked around his cell. Against one wall was a bed. It had probably not been very comfortable even before it had been used by the trotting badgers, but now it was covered with bite marks, and he thought he would just get peppered with splinters if he tried to use it. Shreds of an old blanket had been used to form a kind of nest in one corner of the cell.

'I bet it's full of fleas!' Arthur muttered.

Arthur walked to the bars and looked out. About six feet away lay his doll!

If I could reach it I could speak to Grandfather, thought Arthur.

He lay on the floor and reached as far as he could.

It lay a few feet from his grasp, almost as if it had been positioned deliberately to taunt him. He looked about his cell to see if there was anything he could use to help him. There was nothing.

'This is useless!' he moaned, getting up and kicking the bed against the wall in frustration. After a second or so, there came a distant dull thump in return.

'What was that?'

Arthur waited for a few moments but there were no more sounds, so he kicked the bed again. There was another thump. He didn't think it was an echo, but to be sure he kicked the bed twice in rapid succession. After a couple of seconds came a 'Thump! Thump! Thump!'

He kicked the bed again . . . and the thumping started again, but this time it didn't stop. Arthur pulled the bed from the wall, put his ear to the stonework, and listened. The thumping was coming from the next cell. There was definitely someone—or something—in there. Then Arthur realized that the cell next to him was the one boarded-up. He began to wish he hadn't attracted the attention of its occupant.

The thumping was getting louder and louder. Arthur looked down and noticed one of the bricks in the wall was moving out towards him.

'Oh no—it's coming through!' Arthur panicked. He jumped over the bed then smashed it as hard as he could against the wall, sending the brick shooting back in.

Someone shouted, 'Ouch!' and the thumping stopped.

Arthur pulled the bed back again, and waited.

There was a muffled cry, an even louder thump, and, before Arthur had time to react again, the loose brick flew out of the wall and landed on the floor.

A hand holding a stub of candle appeared through the hole. Arthur froze.

'What's all this noise about? Can't a prisoner get any sleep round here?' came a very grumpy voice. 'I'm the only one allowed to make a din.'

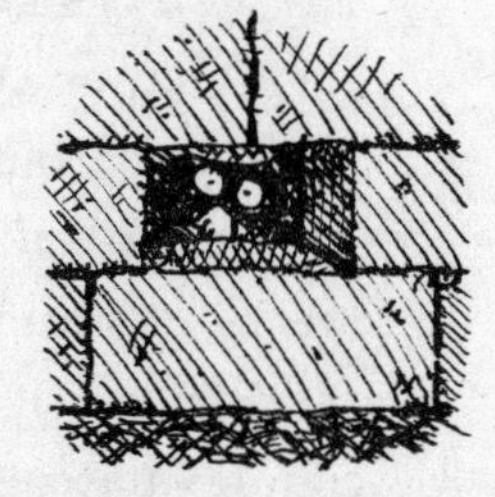

Arthur got down and peered into the hole. A face covered by a mask peered back.

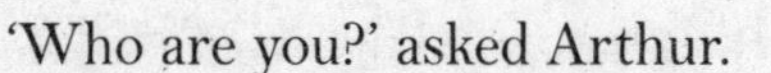

'Who are you?' asked Arthur.

'I am Herbert! And who are you? You are not one of these Cheese Wallahs are you? Can't stand cheese! Used to love it, but you can have too much of a good thing!'

'No. My name is Arthur,' said Arthur.

'Where you from?' said Herbert curtly. 'And what are you doing here?'

'I am from the Underworld. But I've got stuck up here in Ratbridge, and now I've been caught and put in this cell.'

'Blimey. You're in for it. I've heard what they is up to. Blooming evil! You is going to get shrunk!'

Arthur peered through the hole. 'Did you make this hole?'

'Course I did! I make lots of holes. Trouble is that the Cheese Wallahs always come and fill them in again. Never seems to get me anywhere. Been trying to get out of here for years. If I could get these socks off they wouldn't be able to hold me.'

'Socks?' asked Arthur.

'Yes. The Cheese Wallahs shoved me into a pair of iron socks to slow me down. They still don't dare come too close!'

'Why is that?'

'They is scared of me, what with me mask and me walloper. I made me a mask out of a bit of my old boots, and a big walloper out of me bed, and if they come near me . . . wallop!'

'What's a walloper?'

'It's me big mallet! It's great for all kinds of walloping. I love it!'

'You wallop them with it?'

'I wallop everything with it! Trouble is the Cheese Wallahs fixed up a way of stopping me walloping them.'

'How?'

'They stuck these socks on me and a huge electromagnet in the ceiling above my cell, so if I cause any trouble . . . they just turn the magnet on . . . boink! I stick to the ceiling. Blooming iron socks!'

'Is that painful?' asked Arthur.

'Only when they turn the magnet off! I drops to the floor, you see . . . Bonk! But I still usually manage to wallop one or two of them.'

'Why are you locked up here?'

'Me? Can't remember much now 'cause it's been such a long, long time . . . ' Herbert's voice trailed off.

'Do you know what they are up to?'

'Well, I know they are shrinking underlings what they trap and steal,' replied Herbert. 'Don't know why.'

'You say that they're trapping underlings?' asked Arthur.

'Yes, I heard them talking about it when they brought some in. They got some kind of way down into the Underworld from 'ere at the Cheese Hall . . . and they set traps.'

Arthur's mind began to whirr. If there was a route between the Cheese Hall and the Underworld then maybe there was a way for him to get back to Grandfather after all. If only he could get hold of his doll and tell Grandfather what he had learnt, perhaps they could come up with a plan.

Chapter 23

Going Down!

Snatcher climbed on to a table, looking out through the boards that covered the tea room windows. It was raining again.

'Well, is it raining?' asked Gristle.

'No!' Snatcher lied, and climbed back down off the table.

'I still don't like it. It's getting very wet down there. Last time we were up to our knees in water.'

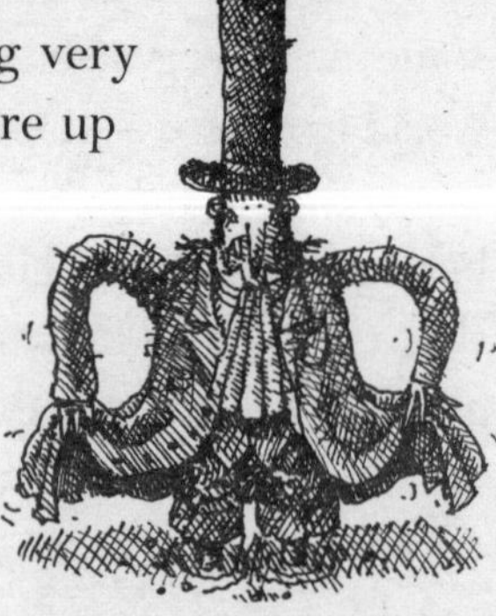

'You worry too much. One more load of them monsters and a few more cheeses, and all will be tickety-boo for our plans for Ratbridge.'

'The traps were nearly empty on the last two trips.'

'I know,' said Snatcher. 'Why else do yer think I got yer to grab them rats, and monsters from the shop? Now get on with yer!' Snatcher fixed Gristle with his good eye. 'Or perhaps I could come up with a substitute for monsters . . . If you get my drift?'

Gristle turned pale. 'No . . . er . . . I'm sure we can find something in the traps.'

'Very good. Just make sure you do!' said Snatcher. 'If you get a good haul, this will be the last time, and then we can seal up the Underworld completely.'

'Promise?'

'Promise!'

The Members looked happier.

'All right then!' Snatcher walked over to a large cupboard and opened its doors. 'First trapping party inside!'

Some of the Members walked forward carrying sacks, and reluctantly entered the cupboard. Snatcher gave them a wink and closed the doors. Then he took hold of a bell pull next to the cupboard and pulled.

'Going down!' he giggled. There was a grinding noise, then muffled screams that faded away. After a couple of seconds there was a distant splash, followed by a bell ping.

'Maybe it is a little wet,' Snatcher smirked. Then he waited for a few seconds before pulling the bell pull again. After a few more seconds there was another ping, and Snatcher opened the doors. The cupboard was empty, apart from two inches of dirty water that ran out onto the carpet. 'Second trapping party, please,' ordered Snatcher.

The Members looked very, very nervous and shuffled backwards.

'Second trapping party, PLEASE!' Snatcher snapped.

The remaining group walked slowly into the cupboard.

'Not you, Gristle!' Snatcher said. 'You can go down on the last load with me.' He turned to Gristle and took a banknote out of his pocket. 'But first I want you to pop down the shops and get me a pair of wellies.'

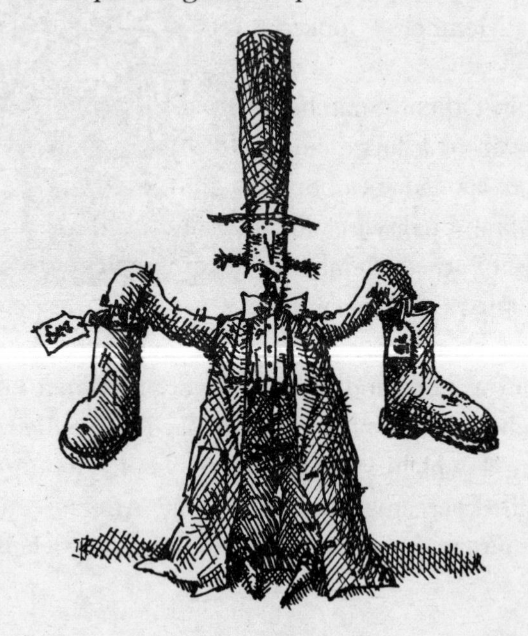

Chapter 24

The Rabbit Women

The crew of the Nautical Laundry, Willbury, Marjorie, the underlings, and the miniature underlings were in the woods, dressed in various sized cardboard boxes. When they'd arrived back at the ship after escaping the Cheese Hall, everyone had been incredibly fearful for Arthur's safety. But the cabbage-heads that Arthur had released from Snatcher's dungeon had explained that they knew where the rabbit women lived, and how to get to their holes. Although very shy, they were only too pleased to be able to help, considering that Arthur had freed them.

They all hoped that the burrows might lead them to the Cheese Hall, so they could somehow get in and rescue Arthur. But rabbit women would never let humans and

rats through their burrows. Fortunately, the laundry had a great supply of cardboard boxes in every size imaginable, and they'd had the idea to disguise themselves as boxtrolls—they thought the rabbit women would be fine with such underlings travelling through their home, as it was something they were used to.

The new cabbageheads wandered about a bit before they found an old oak tree, ran to its base and pulled back some undergrowth to reveal a large hole between the tree's roots. Everybody gathered round as the new cabbageheads whispered to Titus. Titus then whispered to Willbury and Willbury spoke to the group.

'This is the entrance to the rabbit women's tunnels. Our new cabbagehead friends don't want to go any

further.' Willbury smiled at the cabbageheads. 'They are rather frightened of what's happening down there, with all the damp problems, and want to catch up with the other cabbageheads who are apparently making their way to a new cave in the hills. I think it is totally understandable. We don't really know what we are going to find down there. I think we should thank them for bringing us this far.'

The new cabbageheads looked rather chuffed, and gave a little bow. Titus approached Willbury again. When he'd finished Willbury spoke.

'Titus says that he himself would like to stay with us for the moment and help to find Arthur.' Willbury turned to Titus. 'You are very brave, Titus.'

The murmurings in the crowd grew louder, and Titus took Fish's hand. The other cabbageheads took one last look at the hole, waved and disappeared into the woods.

The strange party stood around the hole. It was much, much larger than a rabbit hole, but it would still be a tight fit for a large pirate dressed in a stiff cardboard box. There was an air of trepidation among the group—if the cabbageheads were so frightened of what they would find down the hole, was it really a place that the rest of them wanted to go?

'Who is going to lead the way?' asked Willbury.

There was a pause. Then Fish and Titus put up their free hands.

'Very well,' said Willbury. 'Everybody get out your candles.'

The captain walked over to the hole, produced a box of matches, and lit his candle.

'Right then, me hearties!' he said. 'Form an orderly queue!'

Everybody got in line, with Fish and Titus at the front, followedby Willbury, Tom, Kipper, and Marjorie. One by one, each member of the queue took a light from the captain's candle and disappeared down the hole. Some of the larger pirates took quite a bit of shoving to get them into the hole, but they were all able to manage it without damaging their boxes.

Once underground the tunnel opened out, and even Kipper could stand up and move about with ease. There was a warm earthy smell in the passage.

The procession set off. After a few hundred yards Fish held up a hand, and the procession ground to a stop. Fish turned to Willbury and put his finger to his lips. Then Titus whispered something to Willbury, and Willbury turned to Kipper and Tom.

'Fish wants us all to be quiet, and Titus wants us to put our teeth in. Pass it along.'

They'd made boxtroll teeth from fruit and vegetables, to help further with their disguises. Fish and Titus put their candles down and disappeared into the darkness.

'Aat oo ooh iiink aaye rrr ooht ooo?' Kipper whispered.

'Iiierrrt!' snapped Tom.

After a minute or two, they heard voices from somewhere ahead. The voices grew louder and small green lights appeared. Before long Willbury could make out Fish, Titus, and some other shapes coming towards them. Two rabbit women.

They were both dressed in knitted one-piece suits, with long ears, and they carried glass jars full of glow-worms.

They marched up to Willbury and smiled.

One of them, in a grey suit, spoke. 'Your friend Titus has told us that you'd like us to guide you through our tunnels so you can get under Ratbridge?' Willbury nodded.

Then the other, who was dressed in brown, spoke. 'We'll show you the way but you'll have to be very careful.'

Willbury nodded again, and the rabbit women smiled.

Then the one in brown gave Kipper a funny look.

'You look rather big for a boxtroll.' Then she looked down at Tom. 'And you look rather small.' Titus trotted over to her and whispered.

'Well, Fen, apparently they're a different type of boxtroll . . . just visiting.'

'Oh, Coco, then that explains it!'

'Come this way, please, and remember to be careful!' The rabbit women led the way.

The tunnel soon became lighter, and Willbury could hear more voices. They rounded a bend and were confronted by a wooden door with a notice:

Please close the door after you.
Remember
There are trotting badgers about, and we don't want to lose any of the old folks!

'Mind where you walk!' warned Coco, and then she opened the door.

Through the door was a large, low cavern. Hundreds of jam jars, filled with glow-worms, were tied to roots that hung from the ceiling, and a pale green light fell on the scene below. There were small groups of rabbit women working at looms and spinning wheels, and tending raised vegetable beds. All around them were thousands of rabbits. By each group of workers sat a rabbit woman reading aloud.

Fen turned and spoke. 'Please be very careful not to step on our parents. They are not very bright, but we do love them.'

As the group carefully made their way through the door and into the cavern, Willbury noticed Marjorie was grinning from ear to ear despite her vegetable teeth. She was obviously very impressed by the rabbit women. As

Fen closed the door behind them after shooshing some rabbits away, Marjorie made her way to Willbury, and furtively removed her teeth.

'They're fantastic,' she whispered. 'Just who are they?'

Willbury checked to see that nobody was watching and slipped his teeth out. 'The story I heard was that they were abandoned babies or little girls that fell down rabbit holes. The rabbits took them in and brought them up as their own. It seems to make sense. I guess as they grew up they took charge and now look after the rabbits.'

Despite the working rabbit women not seeming to pay any attention to the visitors, Willbury and Marjorie both quickly put their teeth back in.

Fen noticed Willbury looking at the readers.

'We are very fond of books. You can learn nearly everything from them that rabbits can't teach you.'

Willbury was dying to take his teeth out again and ask questions, but he didn't want to give away that he was not a boxtroll. Instead he listened and tried to make out what was being read. There were some passages from *The Country Housewife's Garden*, some Greek, mathematics, and even bits of *Tristram Shandy* and Jane Austen.

The procession reached a door at the far side of the

cavern and their guides led them through and then closed it behind them.

'We do have to be so careful as we have a real problem with trotting badgers. Last month someone left this door open, and Madeline's step-parents escaped and were eaten. It was very upsetting,' said Coco.

They followed the rabbit women through a maze of passages till finally they reached one that tilted down at a steep angle. The passage emerged in a stone cave and the rabbit women halted. The floor of the cave was awash with water.

Coco held her jar aloft.

'It's getting higher!' said Fen.

'Yes, but it will have to rise a good deal further before it gets close to our burrows. It's the cabbageheads and you boxtrolls that I am worried about.' Coco gave them a concerned look. Then she pointed into the darkness.

'At the other end of this cave is a tunnel that takes you under the town. I am sure Titus and your friend Fish can lead you from here.'

Willbury smiled through his vegetable teeth and bowed in thanks. The others followed his lead.

'No problem. And good luck,' said Coco, and she and Fen turned back up the passage and disappeared.

Chapter 25
The Doll

Back in the dungeon, Arthur was determined to find a way of escaping.

'Do you think you could lend me your walloper?' he asked the hole in the wall.

'You! Borrow my walloper! I should think not!' snapped Herbert.

Arthur pleaded. 'But a doll that I need is in the corridor outside the cell and I can't reach it. I need something to help me get it back.'

'Well, you can't borrow my walloper,' replied Herbert.

'Have you got anything else I could use?' asked Arthur.

'Might have! What's in it for me?'

Arthur thought for a moment. 'If I can get the doll, it might help me find a way out of here. And if I get out, I'll try to get you out as well.'

'Is a bit of string any good?'

Arthur looked across at the doll. 'It might be. How long is it?'

'About six feet.'

'That ought to do it.'

There was a scuffling in the cell beyond the hole and a ball of hairy string appeared. Arthur took it and said, 'Thank you.' Then he unwound it, tied a lasso in one end, and walked over to the bars. After a few attempts he managed to get the lasso around one of the doll's arms and hoist it into the cell.

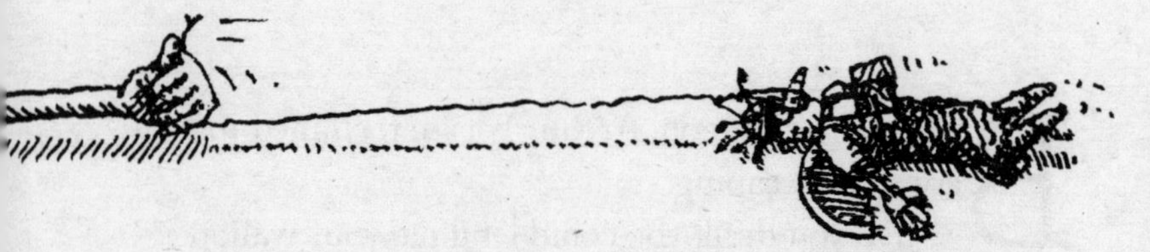

'I've got it!' he cried.

'Can I have my string back?' came a worried voice from the hole.

Arthur unknotted the lasso, rolled up the string, and held it out towards the hole. Herbert's hand darted out and snatched it from him.

Arthur sat on the edge of his bed, and wound the handle on the doll.

'Grandfather! Grandfather! Are you there?' he called.

There was a popping, some static noise, and then he heard what he was hoping for.

'Arthur, where are you?'

'I am locked up in a cell below the Cheese Hall.'

'WHAT!' cried Grandfather. 'They caught you?'

'Well I almost escaped . . . I managed to free the underlings . . . but I couldn't get away from Snatcher quick enough. He accused me of stealing the wings from him!'

'Archibald Snatcher!' Grandfather sounded angry. 'He's up to his old tricks again.'

'I am sorry, Grandfather.'

'You're not to blame. With that shyster involved nobody is safe,' his grandfather said. 'We have to get you out of there. Are you on your own?'

'Well, almost. There is a man called Herbert in the next cell.'

'Pardon? A man called Herbert?' asked Grandfather, sounding astonished.

'Yes!' said Arthur.

'Ask him if his nickname is Parsley!'

Arthur leant down to the hole and spoke. 'Is your nickname Parsley?'

'Don't you know it's rude to call your elders by their nicknames?' came the voice from the hole.

'That's him all right,' came Grandfather's voice. 'Arthur, can you let me speak to Herbert?'

Arthur held the doll out close to the hole. The masked eyes stared at it.

'What are you doing there, Parsley?'

'Is that you, William?' Herbert's voice asked quizzically.

'Yes!'

'What are you doing talking out of a doll?'

'I will tell you later, but you . . . Oh, Herbert, I can't believe it's you. Are you all right? Have you been in that dungeon for all these years?'

'I . . . ' Herbert's voice trailed off. 'I . . . can't remember . . . I am not even sure where I know you from . . . William . . . '

'Oh, Herbert. Don't you remember what happened?'

'No. Not really. My mind is so fuzzy.'

'Don't you remember the fight?'

'No . . . just something vaguely about you, me, and . . . Archibald Snatcher . . . it's all very confused.'

'Maybe if I remind you?' came Grandfather's voice.

'Maybe . . . ' muttered Herbert.

Arthur's grandfather paused for a moment. 'Arthur, you should listen to this too. It's time you heard the truth about why we live underground.'

Chapter 26
Wet!

Several inches of water ran down the tunnels as the procession made its way under the town. Fish and the other real boxtrolls had a way of walking with their feet a few inches up either wall to avoid the water, but even so it dripped down from the ceiling onto their boxes. Willbury and the others were getting very, very wet, and the rats were complaining as the water was soaking the bottom of their boxes.

Tom came to a stop and took out his teeth. 'It's not the water that I hate,' said Tom. 'It's the feeling of the soggy cardboard rubbing on my legs. It feels really horrid, like old wellies.'

'We can do something about that,' said Willbury, taking out his teeth and shouting, 'Large boxtrolls please pick up small boxtrolls and carry them till it gets drier. And you can remove your teeth till further notice.'

'Thanks!' said Tom to Willbury.

The tunnels slowly rose up towards the town, but remained very wet. The real boxtrolls were now in familiar territory, and Fish kept rushing ahead into the darkness and returning excitedly. But after a few of these forays he seemed to grow pensive.

'Have you noticed the pipes?' asked Tom.

Willbury held up his candle to look. There were pipes across the roof. . . and most of them were leaking. Something was wrong.

The tunnel levelled out, and into an area of what looked like very old cellars. They turned a corner to see an iron ladder fixed to a wall in front of them. The ladder disappeared up into darkness. Fish led the way up the ladder and after a short climb they came through a hole on to a dry floor. Wherever they were it was big, as the light from their candles faded into darkness around them. There was a loud click, and above them a light came on. Shoe was standing on top of a huge pile of nuts and bolts, and holding a chain fixed to some kind of glass ball. The light from the ball flooded the cavern. It was full of machine tools, half built pumps, broken bicycles, bits of wire, tools, and pieces of metal of every shape, colour, and description—an Aladdin's cave of engineering scrap.

'The boxtrolls' nest!' exclaimed Willbury.

The boxtrolls nodded.

Marjorie was staring up at the glowing glass ball. 'They've got electric light! Fancy that. I thought it might be possible one day.'

Willbury looked about. 'Where are the other boxtrolls?'

The real boxtrolls looked very sad and unhappy.

Kipper looked at them and whispered, 'I think Snatcher has taken them . . .'

Willbury took this in. 'But it would mean that he must have been capturing them somehow . . . and down here!'

Fish turned to the boxtrolls that Arthur had freed. They just nodded.

Willbury spoke to them very gently. 'You were captured down here?'

The boxtrolls nodded again, pointed back down the hole, and started burbling.

'Could you show us the way up to the Cheese Hall?' They shook their heads.

Titus whispered to Willbury, then Willbury turned to the others. 'Snatcher and his mob put them in sacks after they were captured. But they think he has some sort of mechanical elevator, with an entrance down here somewhere. They say it shot them up to the Cheese Hall. I think we should split up and search for the elevator.

It shouldn't take long with so many of us. We'll meet up here in an hour?'

They split up into small groups and set off. Willbury stayed with Fish, Titus, Tom, and Kipper, while Marjorie teamed up with Shoe, Egg, and some other boxtrolls. As they waited for their turn to descend the ladder, Willbury spoke to his group.

'There is something else. I've got to find Arthur's grandfather. I am very concerned, as he must be running out of food.'

Fish perked up and raised a hand.

'Do you know where he lives?' asked Willbury. Fish burbled something.

'You say you have heard that there are some humans living in a cave off one of the large caverns?'

Fish nodded.

'Do you think you can lead us there?'

Fish looked a little unsure, then nodded again.

'Well, let's try that!' said Willbury. And off they set back down the ladder.

Chapter 27

The Telling

'Herbert. Do you remember growing up?' Grandfather asked.

'No.' Herbert sounded very sad.

'What? You don't remember anything? Don't you remember the Glue Lane Technical School for the Poor?'

'Not really . . . though I do remember the name.'

'Herbert, we grew up in the same street! We played together, got measles together, got in trouble together . . . and got our ears clipped together. Don't you remember burning a hole in my mum's carpet with the toy steam engine we tried to build?'

There was a pause. 'Was the carpet a rather odd green colour?'

'Yes! Yes it was!'

'I do remember something . . . '

'Do you remember us sinking in the canal up to our waists when we tried to cross it when it was frozen?'

'And the ice was so thin in the middle that it cracked and your dad had to pull us out?'

'Yes!'

'. . . It is coming back to me . . .' Herbert said.

'Do you remember Tuesday mornings with the smell of the brewery? And cold nights in winter when the smell of the tannery filled the streets?'

'I loved the smell of the brewery, but the tannery smelt awful!'

At first Arthur somehow felt that it was not his place to be involved in the conversation, but now he asked a question. 'I know there is a tannery, but a brewery?'

'Not any more. It went the same time as the Cheese Industry . . . with the pollution.'

'What happened?'

'Ratbridge was founded on the cheese, but when new industries came to the town, the smoke and waste they produced poisoned the water supply. It got so bad that the local cheeses were decreed unfit to eat, and the cheese industry collapsed. The Cheese Barons went bankrupt overnight.'

'I think I remember that . . .' Herbert said. 'Ain't that the reason Archibald Snatcher turned up at the Poor School?'

'Yes,' replied Grandfather. 'His father was partly responsible.'

'Why?' asked Arthur.

'He ran a mill that had always produced really dodgy cheese. They used all kinds of evil processes. One of their tricks was to boil down cheese rinds, extract the oil, and then inject it into immature cheeses. It was illegal

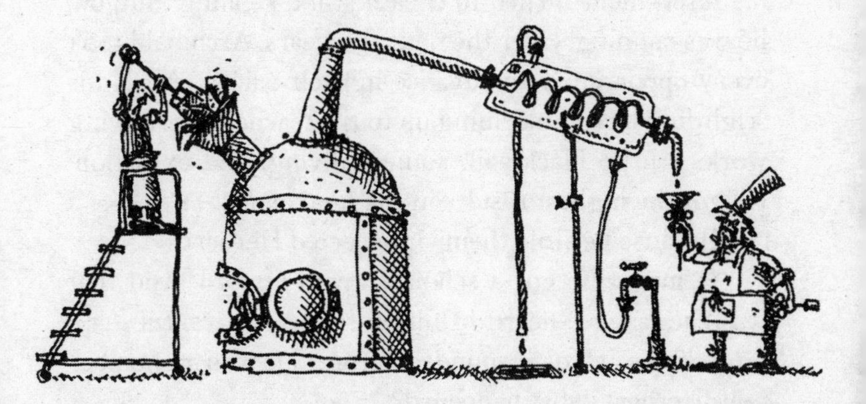

. . . and cruel, but they had got away with it. But as the pollution got worse, making cheese oil was concentrating the poisons. Finally they got sued when they produced the cheese that poisoned the Duchess of Snookworth . . . Archibald's dad lost his fortune and couldn't afford to have dear Archibald privately tutored any more.'

'Oh, I remember Snatcher turning up at school now!' Herbert's memory was coming back. 'He didn't take his fall from Ratbridge society well!'

Grandfather continued. 'Archibald had spent his whole life being waited on hand and foot, so poverty came as a bit of a shock to him. He hated the school, and everybody in it!'

'Why?' asked Arthur.

'He thought it was his rightful place to do what he wanted, and never lift a finger . . . but we didn't play that game,' said Herbert. 'He seemed to think that Ratbridge had done him out of his rightful fortune, and his resentment turned to cheating and stealing. But, oh, he was cunning! Over the next few years, Archibald took every opportunity to advance himself back towards his "rightful place". Smarming up to the teachers, borrowing work, a little blackmail, some bullying, and extortion. He got the highest results in the final exam . . .'

'Because he stole them!' interjected Herbert.

'It meant he got a scholarship to Oxford. And that was the last we heard of him for a few years, till . . .' Grandfather's voice sounded bitter. 'Do you remember now, Herbert, what happened?'

'At the inn?' Herbert replied, slowly.

'Yes, at the inn.'

'Yes . . . some of it is coming back.'

'What did happen?' asked Arthur.

'Herbert and I had just set up as freelance inventors and engineers. We worked in the factories for years, but we had managed to save up enough to start a small workshop . . . One lunchtime at the Nag's Head we heard a raised voice at the next table. I looked over, and there sat

Mr Archibald Snatcher flanked by a couple of heavies.

'"Are you calling me a cheat, sir?" he said to a red-faced man across the table from him.

'"Yes, sir, I am," said the man. "It is not possible to have a hand of cards containing seven aces!"

"It is, sir, for I am very lucky!" Archibald said.

"Well, today, sir, your luck has run out!" And the man at the other end of the table reached inside his pocket. Thinking he was going for a gun, one of the heavies also reached for his pocket, and in an instant the bar cleared, leaving just Herbert and me watching the altercation.'

'Oh, yes!' broke in Herbert. 'The man took out a notepad and asked for Snatcher's name and address. He wanted to report him to the police . . . But he didn't notice that one of Snatcher's men had a catapult . . .'

'That's right,' Grandfather said. 'And that's when

Snatcher gave the order . . . "Administer the treatment!" he said. Something green whizzed across the table and struck the red-faced man in the mouth. The man went pale and slumped to the floor. Then we caught the smell. Oil of Brussels!'

'Oil of Brussels?' asked Arthur.

'It is poison distilled from sprouts. It is very fast acting, and often lethal. They'd shot a small wad of cotton soaked in it down the man's throat,' replied Grandfather. 'Then there was the sound of police whistles outside, and Snatcher saw us. He reached inside a pocket and threw something to me. The very moment I caught it, the bar door swung open, and a group of police officers ran in and saw the man slumped on the floor. Then Snatcher stood up, and pointed at me. "It was him, officer! He has just poisoned that man. Look! He is still holding the evidence." I looked down . . . and in my hand was a bottle of Oil of Brussels.

'The police officers rushed to get me. So I panicked and ran straight through the back door to the street. They followed me, but I was quite fit in those days and I managed to shake them off and climbed down a drain . . . '

'I remember!' cried Herbert. 'You ran out of the door with them after you, then . . . ' he paused for a long time, and then whispered, ' . . . everything went green . . . and I woke up here.'

'But how?' Arthur asked him.

'They must have knocked me out or something, then kidnapped me . . . ' muttered Herbert.

'I knew you had disappeared, because that night I came up out of the drain and found posters up for our arrest for attempted murder. I grabbed some food from a garden, then went back underground to avoid being caught. I knew I would never be safe above ground again unless I could find you as a witness to the truth.'

'Attempted murder? So the man wasn't dead?' asked Arthur.

'No, he survived, but he suffered from permanent memory loss of the event, due to the poison.'

'That's why everything went green. They must have smothered me with Oil of Brussels. That's why me memory is so bad!' Herbert sounded furious.

'And I guess we've both been prisoners of sorts ever since . . . '

'Mr Archibald Snatcher has a lot to answer for,' replied Grandfather.

'So can you help us, William?' Herbert started to ask. But before Grandfather could reply, Arthur heard footsteps.

'Quick! Someone is coming. I'll speak to you later, Grandfather.' He tucked the doll inside his suit, pushed the stone back in its hole and pushed the bed against the wall.

A Member appeared carrying a bowl in one hand and a cudgel in the other.

'Some nosh for you.' He put the plate down, took a key from his pocket, and unlocked the door to Arthur's cell. Then he slid the plate into the cell with his foot and closed and locked the door.

'Take your time, boy! I got to wait for the plate, but I'm in no hurry. They ain't going to be back from the traps for ages.' He sat down, leant against the bars of the cell opposite, and watched Arthur eat.

Chapter 28

A Glimmer at the End of the Tunnel

Fish led the way, and as they walked water washed around their feet. The water level seemed to be rising all the time. Then a sweet and vaguely familiar smell gently wafted into their noses. They'd not eaten for a long time and it was almost too much to bear.

Willbury stopped. 'It's rhubarb! We must be getting close!'

After a few bends in the pathway, a light became visible. Over the rush of water they could just hear music. The music grew louder, and a window and a door became visible in the rock ahead. They reached the door and Willbury knocked.

The music stopped and the door swung open to reveal a short stocky old man with a huge beard and glasses. He looked very damp.

'My word! You're big for a boxtroll!' Grandfather said.

Willbury had completely forgotten he was in disguise. 'I am not a boxtroll!'

'Well, you will do. I have something I need you to help me with—urgently!'

'Of course, we will do anything we can to help. I have spoken to you before, sir. I am Willbury Nibble.'

'Oh! I thought you were a lawyer, not a boxtroll! It just shows that you shouldn't jump to conclusions. But I am pleased to meet you anyway,' said Grandfather.

'It's a disguise,' said Willbury. 'I *am* a lawyer.'

'Are you here about Arthur? I spoke to him just a little while ago. He called me from the dungeon at the Cheese Hall. We have to do something to help him before it's too late.'

'That is why we are here,' said Willbury. 'We believe there is a way up into the Cheese Hall from the Underworld.'

'I see,' said Grandfather thoughtfully. 'I don't know of any such way . . . I also have an idea of how to help Arthur—but I can't do it on my own. I've been hoping for some underlings to come along and help me, but they seem few and far between these days. Can you and your friends help?'

'We will do anything we can. Arthur is our friend and we all want to get him back as soon as we can.'

'Well, do all of you come in,' Grandfather said, taking a step back and gesturing them into his home.

'Thank you!' said Willbury, and they followed Grandfather in.

'If you all like stewed rhubarb I think I might have just enough to go round. Please help yourselves,' Grandfather said, pointing to a saucepan on an old range. 'Then I would appreciate it if you would come through to the back room.'

There was a cheer. Very soon the rhubarb was all gone and they followed Grandfather into the back room

of the cave. There were puddles on the floor and water dripped from the ceiling.

The small room was crowded. At its centre was a brass bedstead covered in a beautiful patchwork quilt. Surrounding the bed was a huge hotch-potch of wires, rods, cogs, pulleys, and other things that Willbury couldn't identify.

'Er . . . What is it?' he asked.

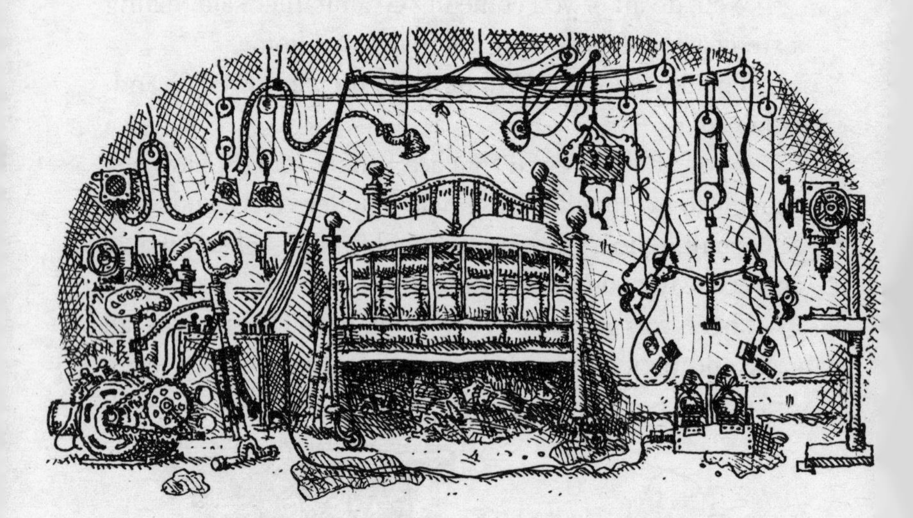

'It's something I have been working on for years. It's finished, but I am too frail to operate it. I think this is the only way we may be able to get Arthur out of his situation.'

'I know just the pirate and rat for the job!' said Willbury.

Grandfather followed Willbury's gaze. 'Are you sure, Mr Nibble?'

Chapter 29

The Keys

Even though the cold porridge in Arthur's bowl was almost solid, he tried to eat it, he was so hungry. Without a spoon he used his fingers to scrape it off the surface of the bowl. It was a very slow process.

'I give up!' Arthur muttered eventually. 'I think I'd rather starve.'

He looked over at the gaoler, who was falling asleep and starting to snore. Arthur coughed loudly, but the gaoler didn't stir. He reached under his suit, and retrieved his doll. He quietly wound the handle, and whispered into the doll.

'Grandfather! Keep your voice down! There's one of Snatcher's mob just outside the cell . . . asleep.'

'What's he doing there?' came a quiet voice.

'He just brought me some food.'

'Did he have to unlock your cell?'

'Yes . . . Why?' 'So he's got a key?

'Yes.'

'Where is it?'

'In his right-hand coat pocket,' Arthur whispered. 'But how are we going to get it off him? He's right across the corridor.'

'Listen, Arthur. I have a plan, but you need to do exactly as I say. Wind up the doll till you hear it ping . . . then give the handle a few more turns until you feel the clockwork can't take any more. But be very careful and don't break the spring!'

Arthur carefully did what he was told, and wound it very gently till there was a ping. Then he carefully wound the handle a few more times until he felt it couldn't go any further.

'OK, I've wound it up.'

'Right,' said Grandfather. 'Reach out of your cell as far as you can, and stand the doll up, facing towards the pocket with the keys in.'

Arthur was puzzled, but did what he was told.

In Grandfather's bedroom underground, Kipper and Tom were ready. Kipper sat on a bicycle that had had its back wheel replaced with some kind of complicated pump. Tom was at the centre of a web of levers and wires that stretched out from all over the room. On his head were a pair of goggles far too large for him. Fixed over the lens of the goggles was a box with wires sprouting from it.

Grandfather turned away from the strange trumpet mouth and spoke directly to Tom and Kipper. 'Can you please get ready . . . and remember what I said to you. You have to work together!'

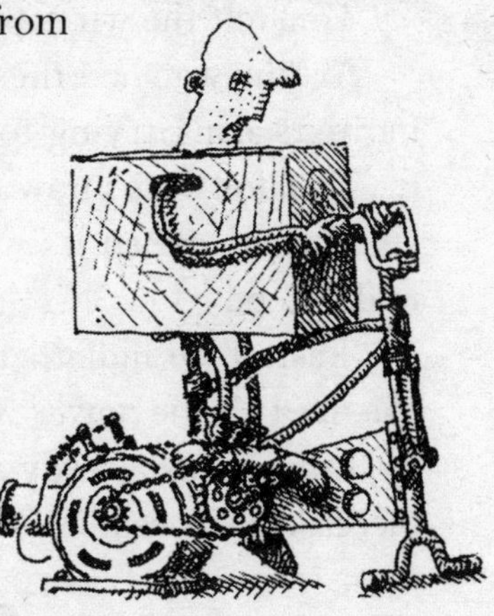

'Working together is what we do best,' replied Tom.

Kipper began to pedal. Soon a humming started to come from the pump, and the levers and wires attached to Tom went taut.

High above in the dungeon, Arthur stood by the bars and stared down at the doll . . . Something was happening! The doll's eyes lit up, and cast two small pools of light towards the coat pocket. Then the doll started shaking and fell over.

In Grandfather's bedroom Tom was cursing. 'It's fallen over,' he said.

'What can you see?' asked Grandfather.

‘Just the gaoler’s boots,’ replied Tom.

‘Use the levers to move the doll’s arms. They should be able to help you get it upright again,’ instructed Grandfather.

Tom carefully started to move the levers. ‘The doll must be moving! I can see all of the gaoler now.’

‘Try moving your legs. The doll should copy your movements.’

Tom felt the wires pull as he started to bend his legs.

Arthur watched the doll in amazement. It started to move its arms, trying to get up on its own!

The doll’s legs now moved as well and it managed to stand again. Then its wings unfolded. Suddenly Arthur understood.

‘Faster!’ Grandfather shouted at Kipper. ‘Pedal faster! We need all the power we can get.’

Kipper was already sweating, but did all he could to increase his speed.

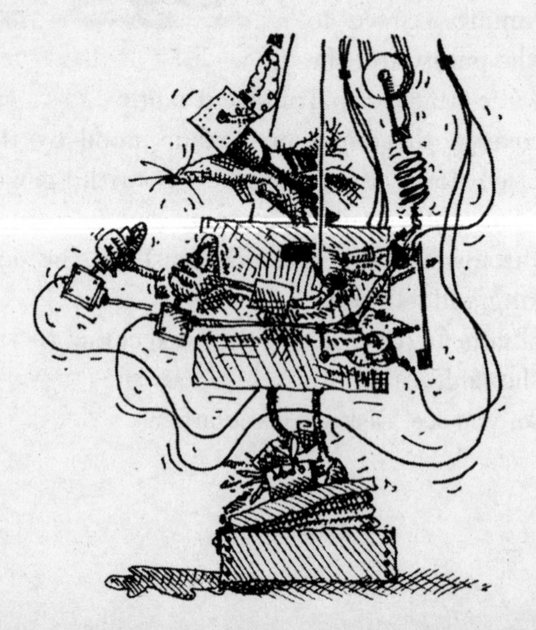

Tom adjusted a knob at the end of one of the levers strapped to his arm.

The doll started shaking as its wings began to beat, then it slowly rose from the floor. Arthur watched as it wobbled and tried to keep upright. The lights from the doll's eyes flicked around the dungeon.

The doll began to fly more steadily. Then it moved slowly across the corridor towards the gaoler. As it reached him, it slowed to a wobbly hover.

'Oh my Gawd! I feel sick!' barked Tom. 'That's it! I can see the pocket. But we need to lose height!'

'Kipper, gently ease off the power,' ordered Grandfather. 'Tom, tell him when you start to fall, and when he needs to increase his pedalling.'

Kipper looked up at him. 'I shall enjoy easing off!'

'Steady, Kipper, steady!' whispered Tom as the doll descended an inch above the pocket. He moved the levers in his hands very slowly and the doll moved forward till its arms entered the pocket.

'A little more power, Kipper!' said Tom, and he started to manipulate the levers attached to his arms. For a few moments there was silence as he struggled to make the precise movements he needed. Then he gave a triumphant shout.

'Got them! Kipper, give it everything you've got!'

Kipper began pedalling ever more furiously, wheezing and panting with the effort.

The doll rose and the keys lifted from the pocket. Tom shifted the controls and the doll turned towards Arthur's cell.

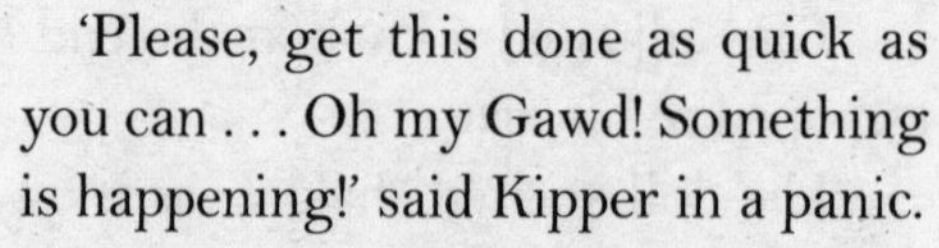

'Please, get this done as quick as you can . . . Oh my Gawd! Something is happening!' said Kipper in a panic.

'Shut up and pedal!' shouted Tom.

But smoke was starting to rise from where the pedals joined the pump.

'Quick! Get the keys to the cell!' Grandfather shouted.

'What's happening?' asked Kipper.

There was a crunching noise, and the pedals seized.

'It's bust!' shouted Grandfather. 'Quick, before it dies!'

In the cell, Arthur stood horrified and helpless as the doll started to fall towards the floor. Tom pushed both of the levers as far as they would go, and the doll tilted forward and dropped into a dive. As it neared the floor Tom pulled the levers back and the doll pulled out of the dive and rushed towards the cell door. Arthur stared. If only it could keep going until it got to him . . .

The doll hit the ground about two feet from the cell. In Grandfather's cave, Tom made one last frantic effort with the levers. Just as it hit the floor, the doll let go of the keys and propelled them desperately towards Arthur. They slid across the floor and through the bars. Arthur picked them up, then reached through. He could just stretch far enough to retrieve the motionless doll.

'Grandfather! Grandfather! I've got the keys!' Arthur whispered in delight, but no one heard him. The doll was dead.

Chapter 30
The Traps

Snatcher and the other Members had been wading around for hours, and were very wet and miserable. They'd found nothing in the traps close to the radiator, so had had to go further afield. Water was everywhere, running over the floor, running down the walls, and gushing from the ceiling. They had to shout to make themselves heard over the sound.

'Maybe we already got all the monsters,' shouted Gristle.

'Remember what I said? You don't want to find yourself in reduced circumstances do yer?' Snatcher replied.

'I think we should check the traps near the elevator again then . . .' Gristle replied.

They made their way back. As they approached, Gristle smiled.

''Ere, guv. We got some!' He pointed to a large net full of boxtrolls.

'My word—and some of them is big 'uns!'

They lowered the net and bundled their haul into sacks. Then they set off to check the next trap, leaving a trail of vegetable teeth floating in the water. To Snatcher's delight and surprise, the next trap was also full of boxtrolls.

'Cor! Get them down, boys!' He rubbed his hands together. 'I'm starting to enjoy this!'

The members bagged up the boxtrolls and moved on. At each trap they found more.

'This is blooming marvellous!' Snatcher chuckled. 'Makes you wonder where they all bin hidin'—we ain't seen so many for weeks! Right lucky for us, but unlucky for them . . . and Ratbridge!'

'Ain't we got enough now?' asked Gristle, struggling under the weight of a sack.

'Let's just check one more trap. It ain't going to hurt.'

'It's killing my back,' complained Gristle.

'That ain't nothing to what it's going to do to Ratbridge!' chuckled Snatcher.

Chapter 31

The Shaft!

Snatcher stood by the open cupboard doors watching as the last of the Members dragged their wet sacks into the tea room. Flashes of lightning threw shafts of light through the cracks in the boards over the windows and across the floor. Outside the rain fell hard on the streets of Ratbridge.

'Take 'em straight down the lab and chain 'em to the railings. . . . Then we'll 'ave a quick cup of tea and some cake.'

The Members picked up the struggling sacks and hiked them off to the lab. There they emptied the sacks out, chained the contents to the railing as ordered, and returned to the tea room.

Willbury looked around the railing, and recognized all his fellow prisoners. There were the crew of the

laundry, Marjorie and the boxtrolls Arthur had rescued, Fish, Shoe, Egg, and Titus, and finally Grandfather. Everybody looked rather battered and very miserable. The ones that had dressed up as boxtrolls now had broken or missing vegetable teeth.

Marjorie was anxiously studying the large funnel that hung above them.

'What is that thing, Marjorie?' he whispered.

Marjorie looked very forlorn. 'It was as I'd suspected! They've built a copy of my machine . . . only much, much bigger.'

'What do you mean?' asked Willbury.

'I had an idea, but when the Trouts turned up with Snatcher, I knew. . . I just knew.'

'The Trouts?' said Willbury, looking puzzled.

'Didn't you see them?' asked Marjorie. 'Two of Snatcher's sidekicks? It was the Trouts, I swear it. They looked pretty rough, but I am sure it was them.'

'So Snatcher has your invention?'

'Yes. It's all these little creatures.'

'What do you mean?'

'The invention that was stolen from me was a resizing machine,' whispered Marjorie.

'A RESIZING MACHINE!' Willbury was flabbergasted.

'Yes—I have discovered how to take the size out of one thing and put it into another.' She pointed upwards. 'It consists of two parts. If you have two things of equal size, one side of the machine drains the size out of one thing and the other part of the machine pumps the size into the other thing,'

'Do you mean it shrinks one thing and makes the other thing bigger?' asked Willbury.

Marjorie nodded. 'See the small funnel over there, on top of the cage by the shed?'

'Yes,' replied Willbury.

'I think that is where they put the underlings to shrink them,' said Marjorie.

'And the big funnel up there?' asked Willbury.

Marjorie looked at the large doors in the floor. 'I'm not sure . . .'

They heard footsteps approaching from the entrance hall and they put their teeth back in. A duck stick appeared followed by Snatcher and the Members, all wearing

ceremonial robes. Snatcher made his way across to the control shed, climbed up the steps, went in, and then spoke through a trumpet device.

'Tonight, gentlemen, we have a special show. Not only do we have enough monsters to finish our project, but also as a finale we shall for the first time use the machine to extract the size from humans. Please get the first boxtroll ready.'

Several of the Members descended on the boxtrolls. Marjorie was the nearest, and so they unchained her and pulled her across the room. She wailed and kicked out, but it wasn't long before the Members had her inside the cage with the door shut. The underlings were howling in despair. Willbury could stand it no longer.

'Stop! This is inhuman.'

The Members turned to look. Snatcher came out of the control shed, and slowly walked down to Willbury.

'Human? What do you boxtrolls know about human?' Then he eyed up Willbury. 'Well, maybe you are a little more human than I thought!'

He put his good eye up very close to Willbury. 'You're not a boxtroll at all, are you? Do you have something to do with that boy we have locked up downstairs? I bet you do!' He chuckled. 'I think I'll have him brought up so you can get shrunk together.'

Willbury froze. If Arthur had escaped then Snatcher had not found out yet! If he hadn't then the longer he stayed away from this machine the better. Either way, delaying Snatcher from sending someone down to get him was a good thing. He changed the subject.

'This machine of yours is rather impressive. What are you using it for?'

'Wouldn't you like to know?' Snatcher grinned.

'By the look of it your plan must be rather good.'

Snatcher puffed up a little as his vanity took over. 'You're right! And I don't mind telling you my plan. We are going to reclaim our rightful place as the overlords of Ratbridge. The Cheese Barons shall rule again!' He laughed madly.

'So how are you going to do that?'

'We are creating a Monster!' Snatcher paused for dramatic effect. 'With your help.' Snatcher laughed again. 'You know we have been shrinking your friends . . . well, have you wondered where the size goes?'

Willbury tried not to look worried.

'AH! You have! Well . . . the size is being put into a very special friend of mine, and as he gets bigger, he becomes more and more unstoppable!'

'Oh!' said Willbury. 'Your special friend . . . do we get to meet him?'

'Yes. Very shortly!'

'And . . . where does cheese come into all of this?' asked Willbury.

'The cheese! Cheese is central to it. To aid our monster's growth we have been force-feeding him a fondue of molten cheese. It goes down very well. A DEEP WELL!' And he laughed at his own evil joke.

'Well, well,' said Willbury.

'Very droll. We have a heated pit that we drop cheeses into. This is piped directly to . . . the Great One. Right down his throat. I think 'e rather likes it.'

Willbury was horrified. What sort of monster could they possibly have created? 'So what happens now?' he said, playing for time.

'The boxtroll in the cage is about to donate some size to the Great One, and after that the rest of you is going to do the same. The Great One will finally be the size we want, and we can unleash him. Boy! Are we going to have fun! I hate this town!'

Snatcher turned and called for a ladder. Soon he was on the top of the shed waving his duck stick wildly in the air.

'To your places, gentlemen!'

The Members moved to positions around the lab tending different machines, and Gristle sat at the controls in the shed. Great whooshes of sound filled the air as the beam engine started to move, then generators started to hum, and power surged through the sizing machine.

'Open the hatches!' Snatcher yelled above the noise.

Trout junior operated a winch in the roof that wound in the chains connected to the doors, while Trout senior inserted a key in the control panel on the rails. Soon the chains were groaning under the strain as they tried to lift the doors.

'More power, Little Trout!' shouted Snatcher.

Slowly the doors lifted and revealed a tiled shaft.

'Bring up the Great One!' screamed Snatcher.

Trout senior turned the key in the panel and a great creaking came from below. Then there was another sound: a hissing, sluggish breathing. It grew louder as whatever it was rose up the shaft. Willbury and the others strained on their chains but they couldn't move.

Snatcher moved to the front of the shed roof and started to peer down the shaft. From his high vantage point he could see whatever was coming. He looked up at Willbury and laughed menacingly.

'You are about to meet my creation. See what I am about to unleash on the world!'

Chapter 32

The Great One!

What looked like a huge jelly covered in filthy grey matted carpet started to emerge from the shaft. As it did the smell of fetid cheese engulfed the lab.

Higher the great grey wobbling jelly rose. Something very long and rope-like was attached to one side of it, and on the other side . . . a pair of hairy door-sized ears came into view.

'It really is a monster . . . ' said Willbury.

The ears were followed by great, red, dinner-plate sized eyes. They swivelled about wildly.

'No!' cried Tom.

Still the creature rose. Its snout, bent and hairy, appeared. Tom was jibbering. 'It can't be!'

There was a loud clunk and the platform stopped as it reached the top of the shaft. Before them was the Great One. A huge bloated creature, larger than an elephant.

'What is it?' wept Willbury

'I . . . I . . . I think it's a rat,' moaned Tom. 'He's from the laundry. It's . . . Framley.'

'YES! What was once Framley is now . . . the Great One!' cried Snatcher. 'Once just nasty . . . Now made monstrous by the hand of man!' Snatcher broke into hysterical laughter for a few seconds, then stopped and turned to Tom.

'I'd been looking for someone really nasty, and when I saw dear sweet Framley in action I realized what a perfect subject he would make.'

Tom was looking ill as his gaze darted between the Great One and Snatcher.

'Now you will witness the fulfilment of my dream.' Snatcher stamped on the roof of the shed. 'Extract the size!'

At the controls in the shed, Gristle threw a lever.

Willbury blinked as there was a flash of blue light from the cage. He realized he could no longer see Marjorie.

'Gristle!' cried Snatcher. 'Give the Great One what he needs!'

There was another flash, but this time from the large funnel above, and the Great One wobbled.

'Next, please!' Snatcher called. 'The boy from the dungeon!'

'No!' screamed Willbury and Grandfather, as one of the Members set off towards the dungeon.

'Oh yes! You'll enjoy watching!' laughed Snatcher, then he called after the disappearing Member, 'And can you bring back one of those shoeboxes from down there. We need something to put all our friends in.'

'You're going to pay for this!' Willbury shouted.

'Quiet!' replied Snatcher. 'Or I'll turn up the voltage and you'll all be reduced to the size of ants!' Willbury fell silent.

Meanwhile Trout senior had opened the door of the cage and groped about the floor inside. Then he stood up with something in his hands.

'Perhaps you'd like to be reunited with your friend?' Snatcher joked. 'Show her to him.'

Trout senior walked around to Willbury and held out his hands.

Standing there was a new tiny Marjorie, about seven inches high, and looking very unhappy.

'Are you all right?' asked Willbury.

'Yes!' came a squeak. Marjorie looked startled by the new sound of her own voice. Then she squeaked again. 'I should never have built the prototype! I just never foresaw the consequences.'

Trout senior looked surprised at the little talking boxtroll, and lifted it up to take a closer look. Just as Trout realized who it was, Marjorie kicked him right in the eye. Trout screamed and dropped Marjorie on the floor, where she ran under one of the machines.

'Get back to your post!' Snatcher ordered Trout. 'We'll let the hounds find it later.'

Trout skulked off. Willbury couldn't see Marjorie anywhere.

'Please, please find somewhere safe to hide,' Willbury muttered to himself. 'I couldn't bear it if you were eaten.'

'Now where is that blooming kid?' boomed Snatcher, as he looked towards the dungeon.

Chapter 33

The Next Victim!

There'd been quite a lot of noise from the dungeon, then heavy footsteps came up the stairs. A struggling Arthur appeared, being held by the scruff of his under-suit. His captor was rather shorter than Snatcher remembered.

'Oi!' shouted Snatcher. 'You've forgotten the shoebox. Bring the boy here, then go and get it.'

As the Member led Arthur through the machines, loud metallic footsteps reverberated around the lab. Snatcher looked puzzled.

Arthur and the Member froze at the sight of the Great One, and Willbury and the others chained to the railings.

'Come on! Come on! We haven't got all night!' ordered Snatcher.

The Member guided Arthur along the pathway towards the shed. As they passed, Arthur was looking worried, but winked, and Grandfather noticed the Member was wearing a mask and was holding something under his ceremonial robes. They stopped on the pathway before the shed.

'What you waiting for?' snapped Snatcher. 'Shove him in the cage, and go and get a shoebox.'

'No,' snapped the Member. 'Get your own shoebox.'

Snatcher was gobsmacked. No Member had ever answered him back.

'What!' he screamed. 'Me! Get my own shoebox?'

'Yes, Archibald!' replied the Member. 'Get your own shoebox!'

Snatcher went red with rage, and almost fell off the roof.

'You . . . ' Snatcher screamed, as he waved his duck stick at the truculent Member, 'are Expelled!'

Suddenly the Member released his grip on Arthur, and threw off his hat and robe. Standing by Arthur was Herbert in his iron boots . . . with his walloper.

The Members froze and Snatcher went very pale.

'Oh my God, he's out! Get him!' ordered Snatcher.

The Members didn't move.

'Get him!' screamed Snatcher. Still the Members held back as they'd all had experience of the walloper, and weren't willing to get within range.

Snatcher was starting to panic. ' . . . All right! . . . all right! . . . Break out the weapons!'

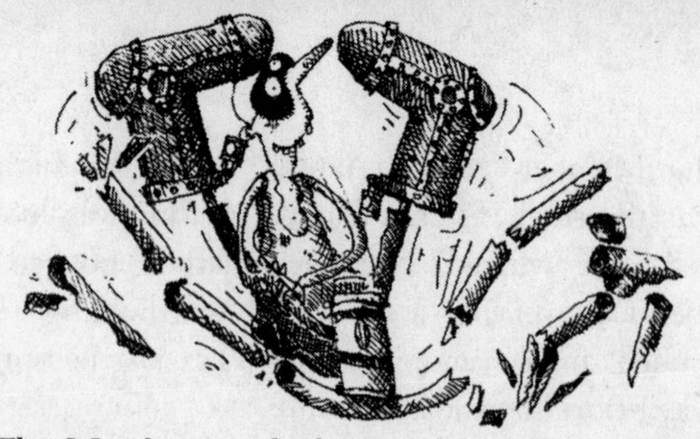

The Members rushed towards a large cabinet on a wall of the lab.

'Smash the railings!' Grandfather shouted.

Herbert looked back at Grandfather and grinned. Then he raised the walloper and brought it down hard.

CRASH! A section of the railing shattered and the Great One started to wobble violently, and let out an awful low moaning. Some of the boxtrolls were freed, and Herbert moved on to the next section. There was another blow and the Great One let out a huge bellow.

'Faster!' screamed Snatcher at the Members, who were fiddling with the cupboard keys.

With two more blows all the railings lay shattered, and the prisoners freed. Arthur ran to his grandfather, and hugged him. Willbury smiled for a moment, then turned and shouted to Herbert.

'Could you bash a hole in the wall so we can get out of here?'

Herbert looked serious. 'Where I wallop is me own business!' Then he winked at Willbury, and made for the wall opposite the cupboard where the Members were now arming themselves with blunderbusses.

Snatcher screamed, 'They're going to get away! Open fire!'

Willbury heard the first shot, and bits of broken cutlery flew over his head. The Members didn't yet have clear sight of the escaping prisoners, as there were so many machines in the way.

'Follow me!' Willbury shouted.

Kipper ran to where Arthur was helping Grandfather, and they took him by both arms, and set off after Willbury.

Herbert reached the outer wall with his walloper. Within seconds a large hole appeared.

'Would you like it any bigger?' he asked the approaching Willbury.

'Why not!' he replied.

Herbert swung his walloper. There was a dull thump, and cracks ran up the wall and a low rumbling started.

'Let's get out of here!' shouted Willbury.

Masonry crashed down as the wall collapsed, sending out huge clouds of dust.

Snatcher danced about on the roof of the shed in rage. 'They're escaping! Shoot them!'

Volleys of marbles, nails, bits of china, even old boiled sweets, clattered as Willbury guided the escapees through the hole. 'Make for the laundry!'

As the dust settled all that could be heard was the sound of rain and distant iron socks on cobbles.

Chapter 34

How Are We Going to Fix It?

'Is everybody all right?' Willbury asked as they arrived on the deck of the laundry.

'I think so,' Arthur smiled. 'But where is Marjorie?'

Willbury looked glum. 'I forgot about her in the rush. I think she must still be trying to hide somewhere in the lab.'

'What are we going to do?' asked Arthur.

'I think we will have to go back and get her. We also have to try to save Ratbridge from Snatcher and Framley—and the sooner we do, the less damage they will have had time to do to the town.'

'We better be quick then,' said the captain. 'I don't really know how we take on Framley now he's so monstrously big, but I suppose we do have to try.' He turned to the crew. 'Gather all the weapons you can find!'

'Can we take off these stupid boxes?' asked Bert.

Fish, who was close by, looked very offended.

'I'm sorry,' apologized Bert, 'but damp cardboard . . . it chafes my legs!'

'OK. Everybody get changed!' ordered the captain.

Kipper raised a hand. 'May I keep my box on?'

'Oh! . . . If you really want to!' replied the captain. Fish smiled at Kipper who smiled back.

'And would you get me out of these darn socks?' pleaded Herbert.

Kipper assisted Herbert with a cold chisel and the walloper.

Soon everybody was ready.

'Do you need shoes?' Willbury asked Herbert.

'Nah! After years in those socks, me feet are as hard as granite!'

Arthur turned to his grandfather. 'Do you realize that now that Herbert is free, you have a witness to what happened? We could clear your name . . . And live above ground.'

'Yes, Arthur, maybe we could. But first we need to worry about Archibald Snatcher and whatever it is he's up to.' He smiled, and then looked more serious. 'I'm not going to stop you from going back with the others to the Cheese Hall, but please think about it.'

'Grandfather, I think I have to go back. I am not sure what's going to happen but I need to be there.'

'All right, Arthur, but . . . '

'I will be careful!' Arthur smiled. 'I haven't come this far to . . . well, you know?'

'Yes, I know,' said Grandfather, and he winked. 'Go on. Off with you!'

Chapter 35

Let's Hit the Town!

As the clouds of dust settled, a smile spread over Snatcher's face. There was a huge hole in the wall of the lab.

'I was wondering how we were going to get the Great One out of here. Ready the armour!'

Some Members pulled dustsheets from a strangely shaped heap. Beneath the covers was a set of iron war armour. It looked like a cross between a giant snail shell and an old riveted boiler. A cannon was fixed above a small platform on either side, and on top in the centre of the back was another platform.

Inside the shed Gristle fiddled with some levers, and a crane moved across the floor to the armour. A hook plucked up the armour and Gristle brought the

crane across. The Members manoeuvred it over the rat. Snatcher climbed down from the shed and inspected the armour for fit.

'It's a bit loose around the edges,' Snatcher muttered. 'We really did need the extra size from those wretched underlings. Gristle, could you lift the armour off for a moment . . . and could the Trouts please check that the extractor funnel is correctly positioned in the cage . . . I am not sure it's working properly . . . '

They did as they were told. Snatcher followed the Trouts, but stopped outside the door. Snatcher snapped the door closed, and locked it.

'Shrink 'em, Gristle!'

The Trouts looked horrified. 'But Masterrrrrrrrrrrr . . . '

There was a flash from above the cage, and the Trouts' cries grew higher and higher pitched, until only an indecipherable squeaking could be heard. Then there was another larger flash from the funnel and Framley wobbled again.

'That should do it!' said a satisfied Snatcher. 'Can we try the armour for size again?'

When the armour was back on the rat, Snatcher inspected it again. 'Marvellous!' he chuckled. 'I knew he'd grow into it.'

The Great One now looked fearsome. The Members took the ladder from the shed and put it up to the platform on the back of the rat. Snatcher climbed up onto it, and a couple of the Members climbed onto the platforms on either side.

'Right, me lads. Gather round. Members of the new Cheese Guild, the time is here!' said Snatcher, perched high on top of the rat. There was a loud cheer. 'The Great One is ready, and Ratbridge is going to pay!' There was an even louder cheer.

'Yes, my brothers! We shall use our Leviathan to overthrow those that have held us down for so long. First we shall remove their government, then destroy the banks, smash their factories, and return Ratbridge to follow an open free trade in cheesy products!'

There was a silence, and then Gristle raised a hand. 'Eh . . . ?'

'We're going to use the big rat to clobber them what done us down, blow up the council offices, rob the bank, knock down the factories, and then start flogging dodgy cheese again!' Snatcher replied.

There was an enormous cheer.

'Right! Let's hit the town!' shouted Snatcher, and he took hold of a pair of reins that had been fixed to the mouth of the Great One, and pulled hard. Slowly his war machine rose and turned towards the broken wall. The Members followed carrying their blunderbusses.

'I've been looking forward to this.' Snatcher smiled to himself.

Chapter 36

Attack on the Cheese Hall

Herbert led the way through the streets of Ratbridge. As Willbury surveyed the little army, he wondered about their selection of weapons. Some of the pirates carried large pants, and were accompanied by rats carrying gunge balls made of laundry waste. This he understood, but the others . . .

The boxtrolls had selected screwdrivers and adjustable spanners, Titus had found a small trowel and a bucket full of gravel, and the other pirates and rats seemed to have grabbed anything that was handy—mops, buckets, old fishing rods. Willbury carried an umbrella that was keeping him dry from the storm that was moving in, and that he thought might be useful in a fight, while Arthur walked by his side carrying the doll.

The thunder drew closer as they stood in front of the Cheese Hall in the rain.

'Right, what's the plan?' asked the captain.

Kipper smiled. 'Perhaps Herbert could "open" the front door for us, and we could creep in that way and surprise them?'

'I don't think there will be much surprise after the noise of Herbert walloping down the door,' said Arthur.

'If we wait for a flash of lightning, count a few seconds, then Herbert wallops the door, the thunder will mask the sound,' suggested Tom.

'That is a very intelligent idea!' Willbury agreed, smiling at Tom.

They waited for a minute or so until the next flash came. Willbury held up a finger, counted for a few seconds, then gave the signal to Herbert. At the very moment the walloper struck the door, a loud clap of thunder filled the street. The front door was reduced to matchsticks.

'Right! Get the mobile knickers ready,' ordered the captain.

Pairs of pirates stretched knickers between them, rats loaded them with the gunge balls, and each pair of pirates was joined by a third pirate who pulled the knickers back ready for firing.

'Everybody keep quiet and follow the knickers,' ordered the captain.

Slowly, the pirates with the loaded knickers made their way up the passageway towards the entrance hall.

As they reached the archway to the hall, one of them peeked round the corner, and signalled that nobody was there. The little army made its way into the entrance hall.

'Prepare yourselves,' whispered the captain. 'I think Herbert should wallop the lab door, and then we let off a volley of knickers . . . ' But before he could finish, the lab door creaked open and everybody froze.

Around the bottom of the door a tiny person appeared. Marjorie.

'I wondered when you were going to get here,' she squeaked. 'But you're too late. They've gone!'

'Thank God you are all right,' said Willbury to Marjorie.

'I am not hurt, but all right is not exactly how I feel,' squeaked a sad-looking Marjorie. 'Six inches tall . . .'

'Well, I am not sure we can do anything about that right now,' said Willbury sympathetically. 'We'd better stop Snatcher and the Members before they cause too much destruction. Do you know where they have gone?'

'They've taken the rat to wreak their revenge on the town. First they're going to destroy the Town Hall, then

rob the bank, and then destroy all the factories!' squeaked Marjorie.

Everybody looked shocked.

'We've got to stop them!' cried Willbury.

'But how?' asked Arthur.

'Knickers and a good walloping!' suggested Herbert.

The crew of the laundry gave a cheer.

'I don't think even that could stop them now,' Marjorie said. 'They have equipped the rat with some really heavy iron armour and cannons. And from what I can see, that rat is vicious and afraid of nothing.'

Everybody fell silent, then after a few moments Arthur spoke.

'Did you say "iron armour"?'

'Yes. Why?' Marjorie asked.

'I have an idea,' Arthur explained. 'There is a powerful electromagnet somewhere above the roof of Herbert's cell. When they wanted to stop him from attacking them, the Members would turn it on, and Herbert's iron boots would stick him to the ceiling. Couldn't we use that? We could pull the rat back here . . .'

Marjorie's eyes lit up. 'It might work.'

'Is the magnet powerful enough?' asked Willbury.

Marjorie smiled. 'It will be by the time I'm finished with it!'

Everybody cheered.

'Could you pick me up and show me your cell?' Marjorie asked Herbert. 'Or rather, the spot just above it? Then we should be able to find the magnet.'

Herbert carefully picked up Marjorie and made towards a space behind the beam engine.

Arthur and the others followed. As Herbert rounded a corner, Marjorie let out a squeak. 'Here it is!'

There was a very large coil of wire on a cart.

Willbury looked puzzled. 'Are you sure? It's just a coil of wire.'

'YUP! That's what it is . . . until you put electricity through it,' Marjorie squeaked with glee. 'We'll be able to give that rat a real surprise! But when we turn it on, we have to make sure the rat comes to the magnet, rather than the magnet going to the rat. We must make sure there is something really solid between the coil and the rat, to stop it moving.'

'How about the end wall of the lab . . . and it is closest to the Town Hall,' suggested Arthur.

'What about all the machinery in here?' asked Willbury.

'Won't the coil be attracted to that?'

'Mmmmmm! You have got a point. We'll have to

fix the magnet to the wall. Some of the loose parts of machinery might fly towards it, but the heavy stuff is fixed down firmly, I think.'

Fish made a gurgling noise, and Titus came forward to whisper to Willbury.

Willbury spoke. 'Titus says the boxtrolls are very good at that sort of thing and would like to help.'

'Very good!' Marjorie squeaked. 'You lot move the coil and fix it to the wall.'

The boxtrolls smiled, and Shoe made a burbling noise.

Titus whispered to Willbury again.

'Would you like to them to rewire the cabling so you can have the switch up here rather than down in the dungeon?' Willbury translated.

'That would be grand!' squeaked Marjorie. 'Could we have the switch in the control shed, please? And wire the coil directly to the generators?'

Shoe nodded, and the boxtrolls set to work. Then Marjorie turned to the captain. 'We need as much power as possible if we are going to stop that rat. Could your crew stoke up the boiler as fast as you can?'

'Be our pleasure!' said the captain. 'We know all about stoking boilers.'

So the crew of the Ratbridge Nautical Laundry set to stoking the boiler of the beam engine. It didn't take long before the great arm of the beam engine was pumping up and down again.

Marjorie asked Willbury to carry her up to the shed, and Arthur and Titus accompanied them. On the bench

at the back of the shed were Arthur's wings and the strange device with two small funnels.

Willbury pointed to it. 'Is that yours?'

Marjorie looked rather awkward. 'Yes . . . Yes, it is.'

Willbury put Marjorie down on the control panel. She took a few moments to study the controls, then pointed to one of the dials.

'That shows the pressure in the steam boiler.' Then she pointed to a lever. 'And that lever engages the generators. Arthur, could you swing it to the upright position, please?'

Arthur obliged. A gentle whirring started and built to a loud hum that filled the whole lab. A needle in another large dial in the control panel started to climb.

'How did they make the magnet work when the beam engine wasn't running?' Arthur asked.

'Arthur, you really are as sharp as a knife.' Marjorie smiled. 'You saw all those glass tanks?'

'Yes,' replied Arthur.

'Those are batteries. They store power, but not enough for what we want. That's why I asked the boxtrolls to wire the coil directly to the generators. Now all we have to do is wait until the needle hits the red.'

'Are you sure that's safe?' asked Willbury.

'Er . . . no,' confessed Marjorie. 'But it should be all right . . . for a bit . . . '

The stokers were doing their work well; the beam engine kept increasing in speed and the generators hummed louder. Soon the needle reached the red.

'Arthur, can you tell the boxtrolls to stand clear of the magnetic coil, please?' asked Marjorie.

Arthur leant out of the door. 'We are going to turn the magnet on. Stand clear!'

The boxtrolls immediately dropped all their tools and ran to the other end of the lab. He turned to Marjorie.

'They're clear!'

'Well then,' Marjorie squeaked to Arthur. 'Would you like to throw the switch?'

Arthur looked a little uncertain.

'Don't worry. What can happen?' smiled Marjorie.

Arthur paused for a moment, and then threw the switch.

Every piece of loose metal in the lab flew towards the magnet. Tools, nuts and bolts, pieces of machinery, the door handle of the lab, bits of chain, and several enamelled mugs and plates whizzed past fearful heads to the magnet, where they formed a jumble on the surface of the coil.

'Strong, isn't it?' Marjorie smiled.

Chapter 37

Magnetism!

Ratbridge was a strange town and had seen some very strange and fearful sights during its history, but none as strange and fearful as that which made its way through its streets now.

At the head of the procession rode Snatcher high on the back of Framley. Following were the other Members, carrying an assortment of blunderbusses and other weapons, and behind them ran the cheese-hounds. Sparks flew out from below Framley's belly as his armour grated on the cobbles of the streets. The noise drew people from their beds, and shutters were thrown open by the townsfolk to see what all the commotion was. Very quickly the shutters were closed and bolted again.

Encouraged by the obvious fear they were generating, Snatcher chuckled to himself. He hadn't felt this good for years . . . or ever!

'Just wait till I get to the Town Hall!' he giggled. His eyes fixed on a rank of shops. About halfway down the rank was a shuttered shop frontage with the three balls of the pawnbroker's sign hanging above it.

'I wonder . . . ?' he muttered to himself.

As Framley drew level with the shop front Snatcher pulled hard on the reins attached to Framley's jaws. The Great One stopped. Snatcher turned to the Members and spoke.

'I can't resist it!' He pulled on Framley's reins and aimed the rat at the front of the shop. 'Go on, my beauty! Let's see what you can do.'

For an uncertain moment the rat didn't move, then he raised his head and swung it at the front of the shop.

The shop did not put up much of a fight. The shutters and windows gave way and the contents of the windows spilled out. The Members let out a mighty cheer and ran forward to gather up the treasures now strewn across the street.

'This is going to be so easy!' shouted Snatcher. 'Help yourselves, boys, there is going to be plenty more where that came from.'

Snatcher pulled on the reins and set the mighty rat off again towards the market square. As they made their way through the streets Snatcher set Framley upon several more unfortunate shops, and each in turn was reduced to a wreck in seconds.

Finally they arrived at the market square, and the Town Hall. Snatcher brought the procession to a halt, and turned to the Members.

'This is where the real fun begins, lads! Prepare to charge!' Snatcher shouted.

'Can't we use the cannons?' Gristle asked. 'I likes a bang.'

Snatcher looked down at Gristle and smiled. 'Oh all right, Gristle. As you have been so good.'

Snatcher gave the order. 'Prepare to fire!'

The Members on the platforms on the sides of the rat took out boxes of matches, and the other Members levelled their weapons at the front of the Town Hall. 'Ready . . . Fire!' Snatcher cried, as he brought down his arm.

There was a roar of cannons and blunderbusses . . . but then something very strange happened. The cannon balls, and the nuts and bolts that the Members had fired, very rapidly slowed . . . stopped . . . and turned back towards the Members.

'Duck!!!' screamed Snatcher. The Members hit the floor as the missiles whizzed over their heads back across the market square in the direction of the Cheese Hall.

Everybody looked very baffled.

'Prepare to fire!' Snatcher screamed again.

The Members tried to follow orders but now their guns and ammunition were pulling them back towards the Cheese Hall.

'Master . . . ' cried a very frightened Gristle. 'Something weird is 'appenin' . . . '

'Stand firm!' ordered Snatcher, but the terrified Members were now letting go of their blunderbusses, and untying their ammunition bags from their belts to avoid being dragged across the square.

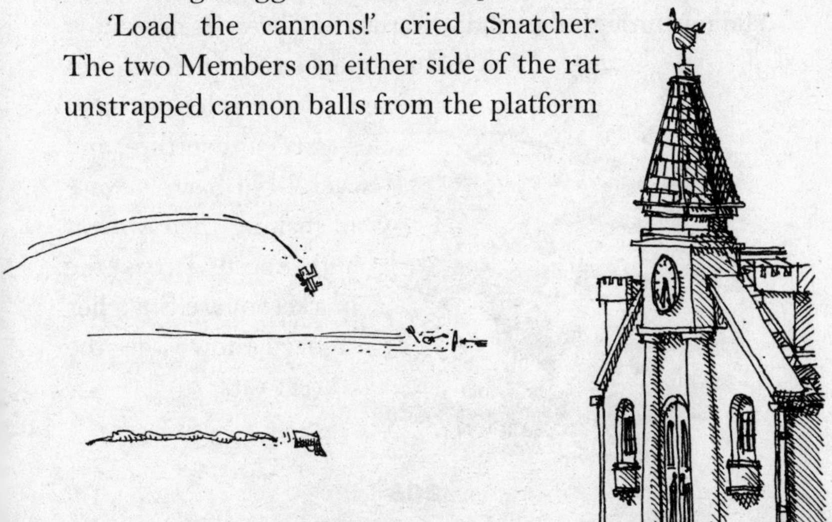

'Load the cannons!' cried Snatcher. The two Members on either side of the rat unstrapped cannon balls from the platform floors, but before they could load them found themselves dragged off the platforms. They disappeared across the square, screaming.

'It's a curse!' cried a Member.

'Run!' cried another. And the Members ran in all directions.

Many people in Ratbridge might well have been very frightened by the noise of the blunderbusses and cannons, if it were not for the fact they had problems of their own. In every household, objects were coming to life.

Saucepans and cutlery had suddenly decided to stick to walls, and cooking ranges and iron bedsteads were going for walks. Several ladies who had slept in their steel reinforced corsets now found themselves irresistibly drawn to join the saucepans and cutlery. One man who had invested in an expensive set of metal false teeth found himself hanging on as tightly as he could to the kitchen table to avoid being dragged through the house, while outside in the street, dogs with studded collars found themselves sliding through the mud towards the Cheese Hall.

Snatcher looked completely flummoxed. A cart, riderless bicycles, garden furniture, and several old barrels were all making their way at high speed across the market square. Snatcher looked down at the great rat.

'It's down to us, Framley! Attack!'

The Great One let out a low moan.

'Come on, my horrid!' cried Snatcher.

Framley seemed very perturbed. His legs were scrabbling on the wet cobbles, but he and Snatcher were not moving forward . . . in fact, they were starting to slip backwards . . .

Inside the lab Arthur and the others were feeling a little nervous about the strange noises that were coming from outside. Distant whizzing or clattering grew louder very quickly, then stopped suddenly with a thwonk, thud, or similar.

'Do you think we'd better go and have a look at what's happening?' Arthur asked Tom.

'I think we know what's happening, Arthur. I think we'd better stay safely in here. If the metal doesn't get us, there are going to be some very angry people out there.' Tom winked.

Snatcher turned around to see the last of the cannon balls fly off across the square. The rat was picking up speed, despite desperately trying to cling on to the cobbles with its claws. There was a horrible scraping and grinding as the armour slid across the market square.

'Oh, my poor horrid!' Snatcher muttered as Framley let out a mournful whimper.

On the way to the Town Hall Snatcher had taken what he thought was the most direct route, but he now discovered that there was an even shorter route back . . . a straight line.

As the armoured rat reached the edge of the market square, it was not a street that they met but a cobbler's shop. Snatcher crouched down on the back of the ever-accelerating rat and hung on as a crashing rang out and they disappeared through the shop frontage, leaving a large armoured-rat-shaped hole. In the apartment above the shop, there was much surprise as a screaming crouched man on a small railed platform came through the wall, moved rapidly across the room, and out through the back wall. The Great One then slid across the muddy back garden till it reached the next building, and disappeared again.

The armour protected Framley as they smashed through badly built building after badly built building, but Snatcher was getting rather bruised.

Finally, with a great deal of splintering and crashing of masonry, Framley broke from a cake shop across the road from the Cheese Hall, shot across the street, and hit the lab wall in a puff of flour and cake crumbs.

The building shook.

'I think someone's arrived!' Marjorie squeaked.

Arthur wanted to see what was happening. He ran down to the floor of the lab and found a wooden step-ladder, placed it below a window near the magnet, and climbed up. After a few moments he turned and shouted.

'It's Snatcher and the rat! And they both look really angry . . .'

'We'd better keep them there then,' replied Willbury.

'I'm not sure you want to do that!'

'Why?' shouted Willbury.

'Because Framley looks like he could burst at any moment!'

'Can we just reduce the strength of the magnet, Marjorie?' asked Willbury.

Marjorie looked unsure. The stokers were still very enthusiastic, and the generators were spinning faster and faster.

'The circuit is either on or off. The only way we can ease the power off the magnet is to slow down the generators, and that's going to take a few minutes even if we stop stoking the boiler and let off some steam . . . !'

'Quick!' shouted Arthur. 'Framley could blow any second . . . '

Willbury turned to Marjorie. 'Well?'

'We could turn the current off for a few seconds . . . ' Marjorie suggested.

'Do it!' snapped Willbury.

'Herbert! Can you turn off the switch?' Marjorie squeaked.

He leant forward and reached out but then pulled back from the switch. 'I can't! It's red-hot.'

Willbury wrapped a handkerchief around his hand and tried. It was useless . . . with all the current the switch had fused solid.

'We have to get everybody out of here!' cried Willbury. 'An explosion could bring down the rest of the lab. Everybody out! Don't use the hole in the wall! It's too close to the rat! Use the door to the entrance hall.'

Willbury carried Marjorie, and he and Titus, the stokers, and boxtrolls all ran for the entrance hall, but as Willbury reached the door he turned to see Arthur making for the shed.

'Arthur! What are you doing?' he shouted.

'I've got to get my wings,' Arthur shouted back, running up the steps to the shed and in through the door. He grabbed his wings and hastily strapped them on, winding the handle on the wings' motor as fast as he could. Then he grabbed Marjorie's prototype from the bench, and made for the door.

Over the noise of the machines in the lab he heard Willbury calling him.

'Arthur! Arthur!'

Arthur turned to see the last of the underlings and laundry crew disappearing out of the door past Willbury.

Arthur ran out of the shed, adjusted the knob on the front of the box, pressed both buttons, and jumped.

Chapter 38

The Big Bang

The day was not going well for Snatcher, and now it was raining water from above and small metal objects from every other direction. How could things get worse?

Beneath him the Great One's armour was now looking rather battered and flimsy and the rat was bulging out round the edges of the iron suit like a squashed balloon. There on the ground right beneath Framley's head, in the midst of a pile of rubble and cake crumbs, was a cream bun. It was not a large cream bun, but it would do until he could get more cheese. Framley had not eaten since he'd had his last dose of 'size', and even though he was extremely uncomfortable he felt rather hungry. He reached down, snapped up the bun, and swallowed. What followed was disastrous.

A clap—like thunder—broke as Framley burst and everything went yellow!

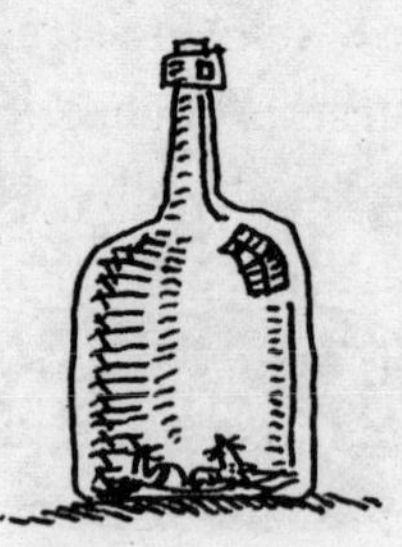

Chapter 39

Skinned!

Arthur flew straight towards the lab door. Just as he was about halfway across the entrance hall, he remembered the two mice in the bottle. He turned and landed by the door of Snatcher's suite, ran in, grabbed the bottle from the table, ran back out of the door, and then across the hall through the archway. At that moment he was hit by a blast from behind.

The blast shot him through the door, towards the windows of the inn, and he felt someone suddenly grab him out of the air and pull him to the ground. Then came something thick and very sticky, and everything went silent.

Arthur tried to stand up. He was under some kind of soft elastic yellow tent. With a slight struggle, he freed his hands, and then with one finger he managed to poke a hole through the yellow skin. He stretched the hole until he could step out of it. Strands of cheese hung from his wings.

He was standing in a shiny yellow street. Everything was covered in the smooth film of elastic cheese. Arthur turned towards where the Cheese Hall had once stood. Now there was just a low, shiny, yellow mound. The buildings around the Cheese Hall all now had yellow frontages, but didn't seem to be damaged (apart from the bakery).

Arthur looked about on the ground close to where he stood. Odd shapes were wiggling under the cheese skin, and he recognised the form of Willbury, laid flat with outstretched arms. Arthur ran and started to peel the cheese film away from his friend.

'Willbury . . . Willbury . . . Are you all right?'

A muffled grunting came through the skin. Soon he had Willbury freed.

'Thank you, Arthur!' said Willbury as he tried to disentangle cheese strands from his wig.

A splutter came from his hand. 'I hate cheese!' squeaked Marjorie.

Within a few minutes, everybody was unpeeled and had gathered together. They all looked rather shocked, but happy, apart from the captain and the boxtrolls, whose boxes were now so damaged by the rain and the blast that they were embarrassed to be seen in them.

Arthur remembered the bottle and ran to where it lay, still under the cheese. He broke through and saw that the bottle was smashed. Close by, the bodies of the two tiny mice lay on the ground.

'Captain! Quick!' Arthur called.

'I think it's Pickles and Levi!'

'You're right . . . I would recognize them any size,' said the captain, rushing over. 'But they're not moving . . . and they are not quite the right shape . . . sort of swollen up around the belly . . .' His eyes lit up. 'They're breathing!'

Levi and Pickles started to move and let out little groans.

'They must have gorged themselves on the cheese,' the captain said, smiling, and then carefully placed them both in his pocket.

'What do you think has happened to Snatcher and Framley?' asked Arthur.

'I think we can guess what has happened to Framley,' said Willbury, surveying the cheese. 'But Snatcher? I think we'd better go and look for him.'

Willbury led the group over the mound that had once been the Cheese Hall, towards where the back wall of the lab had stood. Large pools of water were collecting on the surface of the cheese. They started to look about for signs of Snatcher.

It wasn't long before a new noise started—a low rumble they could feel under their feet. Arthur turned towards the mound and noticed ripples running over the surface of the pools of water.

'Look, Willbury! Look at the water!' Everybody turned to stare.

Beneath the town, the water had been doing its work. The foundations below the Cheese Hall had been almost completely washed away and, combined with the shock from the explosion, it was just too much.

'Quick!' shouted Willbury. 'Get back!'

The rumbling grew louder, and the mound was starting to shake.

Having retreated quickly, they just stood and stared as there was a huge cracking noise and the mound suddenly disappeared.

In the same moment, all across the town, the iron plates covering the holes to the Underworld were blown high into the air, and in the woods the trotting badgers were shot out of their tunnels.

Fortunately for the rabbit women, the doors they had constructed to keep the rabbits in were very well built, and saved them from the blast.

Quiet returned and everybody moved forward to look down the hole. It was some twenty or thirty feet deep and lined with the skin of cheese. Water was washing about in the bottom.

'It's a big hole!' said Kipper. 'Like a yellow swimming pool.'

'What's a swimming pool?' asked Arthur.

Willbury smiled. 'I think we had better get back to the ship to see if your grandfather and the others are all right. Kipper can show you what a swimming pool is later.'

Then Willbury noticed how forlorn the boxtrolls looked.

'I am sure we can find a few new boxes; if not I shall have some made!' The boxtrolls beamed, as they had never had brand new boxes.

'It's all very well for them,' said Marjorie. 'But what about me, and the other shrunken creatures?'

'Hang on a minute!' said Arthur, remembering the prototype. He rushed back around the edge of the hole to where it lay under the cheese skin. Arthur peeled back the skin and lifted it up carefully.

He ran back to the group and heard Marjorie squeak with delight. 'Oh, Arthur, thank you, you've got my sizer!' Then she looked glum. 'But I don't know where we'll get my size back from without Framley.'

'There must be somewhere to get it from,' said Arthur.

'Maybe,' said Willbury. 'We'll have to think.'

As they set off for the ship the townsfolk were just arriving to find out what all the commotion was. They gawped at the newly decorated hole and buildings. The underlings had been through so much that now even Titus held his cabbage up in a very un-cabbage-head way, and walked straight past them.

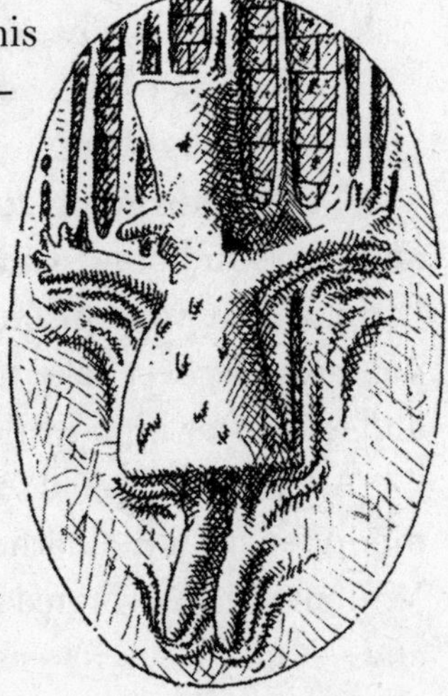

But what nobody noticed was that high above, just under the gables of the bakery, was what looked like a ship's figurehead of a very angry man wearing a top hat. The figurehead started to slide slowly down the wall.

Chapter 40

Repairing the Damage

Weary, and covered with bits of sticky cheese, but feeling proud and relieved, the group arrived back at the laundry.

Grandfather beamed when he saw them, and Arthur gave him a huge hug.

'I think it's going to be safe for you to set up home above ground now,' said Willbury. He turned to Arthur. 'I think that your grandfather is very tired. Why don't you and Herbert take him down to the captain's cabin, and look after him, while I get a few things sorted out.'

'All right,' replied Arthur as he turned and looked fondly at his grandfather. Then Arthur turned back to Willbury. 'I am worried about where we are going to live, and—'

Willbury cut him off. 'You are not to worry about that. I have an idea. You concentrate on looking after Grandfather. I am sure he has missed you and it would be good for both of you to catch up.'

For the rest of the day Arthur sat by Grandfather, listening to stories of Herbert's and Grandfather's youth. There didn't seem to be anything wrong with Herbert's memory now as story after story unfolded, and Arthur could hardly bear to tear himself away from them, but they kept needing fresh top ups of cocoa and biscuits from the galley.

There were tales of learning to ride bicycles, disastrous experiments, of pet frogs and engineering projects.

In the late afternoon when they were all growing sleepy, Grandfather turned and spoke to Arthur.

'I am glad we have come above ground. I loved every moment I spent living in the Underworld with you, but it's not the best place for a child to grow up in. You need sunlight, and you need friends. And now you are going to have both.'

Arthur smiled, and a quiet calm settled on the cabin as they drifted off to sleep.

About seven o'clock there was a knock on the cabin

door and Arthur, Grandfather, and Herbert awoke to see Kipper's face, smiling and covered in splashes of paint.

'If you would like to come through, Willbury has called a meeting in the hold.'

'Why have you got paint all over you?' asked Arthur.

'You'll just have to wait and see,' replied Kipper.

Herbert and Arthur went to help Grandfather up but before they got to him he had stood up on his own.

'Come on, then,' said Grandfather, 'let's get to the meeting.' And he set off. Herbert and Arthur grinned at each other then followed.

When they arrived in the hold Willbury was sitting behind the ironing board with the captain. In front of him lay the prototype resizing machine and Arthur noticed Marjorie almost hidden behind it.

He also noticed that quite a few of the pirates and rats had splodges of paint on them.

'My dear friends,' Willbury began, 'there are a number of important issues to resolve.' He turned to Grandfather. 'I have already taken the liberty of asking my landlady if she would rent the vacant rooms above my shop to you and Arthur. She agreed and this afternoon I had Kipper lead a working party to clean and repaint the rooms. There is even a small boxroom that Herbert could use till he gets his own place. You are welcome to move in any time you like.'

Grandfather smiled from ear to ear and called to Arthur, 'What do you think?'

'Yes, please!' answered Arthur with a huge grin. Kipper and Fish both patted him on the back.

There was a roar of approval from the meeting and then Grandfather spoke. 'I want to thank you from the bottom of my heart . . . but how are we to pay the rent? I don't have a job and I haven't got any savings.'

'You're not to worry about that. I have filed a claim for compensation, on your and Herbert's behalf, with the clerk of Ratbridge courts, against Snatcher and the Cheese Guild. Until it comes to court, if Arthur helps out with chores, I'll sort out the rent.'

There was another cheer. Willbury raised a hand and spoke again. 'Now we come to our friends the underlings. The problem of the entrances to the Underworld has been solved, but . . . at the moment most of the Underworld is flooded. Does anybody have any suggestions?'

Marjorie stood up on the table and squeaked, 'Easy!'

'Yes?'

'We already have a beam engine on this laundry. Pumping water is what they were built for. All we have to do is drop a pipe down into the Underworld and pump out the water.'

'I might be being stupid,' said Willbury, 'but where are we going to pump the water to?'

Kipper raised a hand. 'How about the hole where the Cheese Hall was? That cheese seems to be pretty waterproof and would stop it leaking back into the Underworld.'

'Would it work?' Willbury asked Marjorie.

Marjorie thought for a moment. 'I think so . . . and once the underground becomes drier the boxtrolls could repair their drainage system to stop it flooding again.' The boxtrolls made gurgles of agreement.

Kipper raised a hand again. 'Can I help them?'

'I see no reason why not,' Willbury said.

'Well, that just leaves us with one last problem. Size! We have our friends here who have been reduced in size, but we know there are many others, and some in the hands of those who just treat them as pets. We have to get them back, and we have to work out where to get the size to put them right. Does anybody have any suggestions?'

'How about we find the Members what ran away, and suck the size out of them?' Bert suggested. There were cheers from the pirates and rats.

'I'm sorry but I'll not countenance revenge shrinkings. We must not lower ourselves to that. No, we must find another way.'

'Couldn't we use vegetables to suck the size from?' asked Tom.

Titus looked shocked, as Marjorie raised a hand to speak. 'You have to use living creatures. If you used vegetables it would be very dangerous and you might end up with some strange results.'

'What, like half trotting badger, half potato?' asked Kipper.

'Yes,' replied Marjorie.

'Might be an improvement,' suggested Tom.

'Couldn't we all donate a little bit of size?' asked Grandfather.

'You could, but with all the creatures we have to resize it would leave you all pretty tiny if it were to make any difference,' replied Marjorie rather sadly.

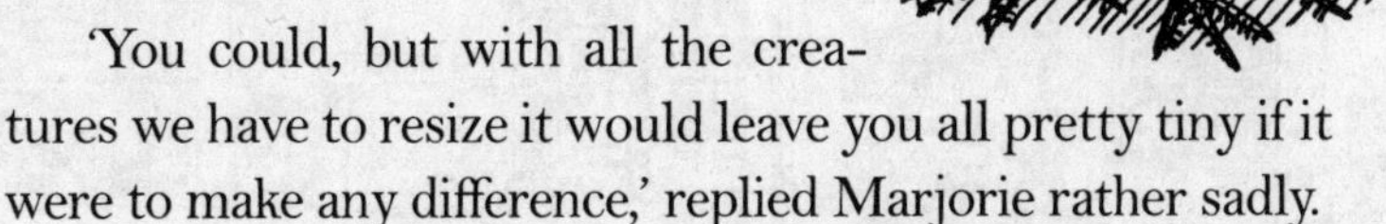

'Well, let's think on it,' said Willbury. 'And there is the issue of how we first get the other underlings back to resize them. They're in homes all over the town. If we steal them back we are going to start another whole round of trouble, and with the court case coming up that is the last thing I want.'

The hold fell silent and everybody looked rather glum. After a few minutes Willbury spoke again.

'Let's get some rest. It has been a tiring few days, and I am sure we'll think better after some sleep. We can all meet up here tomorrow morning to start pumping out the underground. For now, those that are coming back to the shop please meet me up on deck.'

A few minutes later Arthur found himself on deck with the boxtrolls, Titus and the tiny cabbagehead, Grandfather, Herbert, Marjorie, and Willbury.

They set off, and soon arrived at the shop. Willbury opened the front door and stopped in his tracks.

'Oh, my word!' he exclaimed.

The shop was cleaner and tidier than Willbury could possibly have ever imagined. The walls and ceiling had been given a fresh coat of white paint, the old bookshelves had been righted and repaired, and were tidily stacked

with all his books, the floorboards had been swept and polished, and against one wall stacked soap boxes formed open-fronted storage spaces into which the rest of Willbury's loose possessions had been neatly piled up.

There was a popping noise and Willbury turned towards the fireplace. He smiled. In front of the fire was his old armchair . . . and it had been repaired.

Willbury took a key off his keyring and handed it to Grandfather.

'This is a spare key to the front door. Please feel free to wander through here whenever you like.' Then he turned to Fish. 'Would you like to show our friends their new home?'

Fish smiled at Arthur and led them through the door at the back of the shop into the hallway. Where once the hallway had been dark and dingy, it was now bright and clean. A lit ship's lantern hung from the ceiling, and every surface was painted white. Fish noticed there was something different about the back room as well. He ran down the hall and gave a gurgle. Arthur, Grandfather, and Herbert followed.

The back room looked like a new ironmonger's shop.

Cubby-holed shelving made from cardboard now covered the walls, and all the nuts and bolts that had been on the floor had been sorted and placed in different labelled holes.

Fish let out a whistle, then stopped still. There was a stack of folded . . . clean . . . brand new . . . cardboard boxes on the floor. He bent down to stroke the top box. Then he turned and let out an enormous gurgling cry.

There was a scrabbling of feet from the shop and the other boxtrolls rushed past Arthur, stopped, and hooted at the sight of the boxes. Fish came forward and

gently shooed Arthur, Grandfather, and Herbert out of the room and closed the door. As soon as the door was shut, there was a frantic tearing of cardboard, and whooping, followed by some chewing noises, then the door opened again. Fish and the other boxtrolls were wearing the new boxes and grinning from ear to ear.

Fish swaggered along the hall and marched up the stairs, waving for Grandfather, Arthur, and Herbert to follow. At the top of the stairs Arthur ran ahead. There were three doors. He opened the first one to a tiny room with a hammock and another cardboard box. But this time the cardboard box had been tipped upside down to form a table. On it was a small vase of flowers and a cake.

'Is this my room?' he called over his shoulder.

'No, that is the boxroom for Herbert.' Arthur smiled and opened the next door. There he saw a brass bed, and tools laid out on a workbench.

'Is THIS my room?' he asked.

'No!' came Willbury's voice. 'It's Grandfather's.'

'I do hope so,' said Grandfather. He walked forward, looked at the bench, then sat on the edge of the bed and smiled a huge smile.

Arthur then turned to the last door. 'Then this MUST be my room!'

The room was a little smaller than Grandfather's and was painted completely white, including the floor. There was a cardboard box table like in the smaller room, but there were also some shelves. On the top shelf, lying on its side, was a large bottle. And inside the bottle was a model of the Ratbridge Nautical Laundry—complete with tiny washing. Arthur noticed a small plaque fixed to the bottle which read, 'To Arthur from the R.N.L.'. Arthur beamed and then Herbert spoke.

'Kipper had been making it since they arrived in Ratbridge, and when he heard that you had lost all your toys, he decided you would make a good home for it.'

Arthur felt very touched. 'I shall treasure it always.'

Arthur looked about the room again and saw a hammock, which he jumped into and lay down. It felt very comfortable apart from a bump behind his neck. He reached his hand round and to his surprise he found his doll. Arthur was confused. He checked to see if he had another doll under his suit, but discovered it was not there.

He swung himself out of the hammock and ran next door to his grandfather.

'My doll? It was in . . . ah . . . my room!'

'Tom found it and knew that it was broken,' Grandfather explained, 'so he brought it to me. I asked Marjorie if she could fix it this afternoon.'

Arthur smiled and held up the doll.

'I'm afraid that it will never fly again, but you will be able to speak to me through it in a few weeks after I have got to grips with these new tools.'

They smiled at each other, and Grandfather spoke again.

'I think we are going to be happy here.'

'Cocoa!' came a call from downstairs.

'Yes . . . yes we are,' said Arthur.

Chapter 41

Measure for Measure

The next few weeks were very busy for Arthur. Grandfather thought it would be a good education for him to help with all the work that had to be done, so each morning Arthur would set out for the laundry and help out. Some days, under the guidance of Marjorie, he would help the crew of the laundry pump out the Underworld, and on other days he would work with the boxtrolls as they rebuilt the underground drainage system.

Meanwhile, Willbury, Herbert, and Grandfather spent their time preparing the compensation case against Snatcher and the Cheese Guild. When the day of the trial came, neither Snatcher, nor any Member of the Cheese Guild, turned up to defend themselves, and the court awarded the hole in the ground to Herbert and Grandfather (as it was the only property that Snatcher and the Cheese Guild owned).

That evening after dinner, everybody who lived in the shop went for a gentle walk to view Grandfather and Herbert's hole. As they approached it they noticed local children swimming in it.

'I think you are going to have to fence off your hole,' said Willbury. 'What would happen if a child got into difficulty?'

'Seems a pity,' said Grandfather. 'I suppose we could pay one of the pirates to keep an eye on the kids . . . But where would we get the money to pay him? We still have not got even enough money to pay you rent.'

'Why don't you charge for admission?' asked Willbury.

Herbert and Grandfather agreed this would be a good idea, and it was soon agreed that the laundry would provide lifeguard cover every day between six a.m. and eight p.m., and that they would also help erect a fence around the pool to stop any accidents. Any spare hot water left over from the laundry would be piped into the pool.

The 'Ratbridge Lido' became the main attraction in the town. Children would swim there by day, and in the evening when it wasn't raining the fashionable women would parade along its shores, while the pirates would have raft races. Herbert, who enjoyed swimming very much, taught Arthur how to swim and once the water became warm, Grandfather could be found taking a dip most days.

All this time the question of the shrunken creatures had not been solved, but then something happened.

A Frenchwoman arrived in Ratbridge and found work in one of the cafés that had sprung up around the Lido. She immediately became the centre of attention for the fashionable women, as she was from 'Pari'.

Arthur was walking past the café one day after a swim when he heard a woman—Ms Hawkins—ask the waitress, 'May I ask you about the Pari fashions, my dear?'

'Certainly. What do you want to know?'

'Is it true that hexagonal buttocks are going to be the rage this year?'

'*Quel horreur!* What is it with zee Ratbridge ladies and their fascination for ridiculous buttocks?'

Ms Hawkins dropped her pet boxtroll and fainted.

As Arthur fetched her some water, an idea came to him.

'Meet me at the Nautical Laundry tomorrow morning with the other ladies?' he said. 'I think I have the solution to your large . . . erm . . . behind problem.'

The dazed lady smiled at Arthur and nodded.

The next morning, Arthur was waiting eagerly on the deck of the laundry, after explaining his plan to Marjorie.

As the lady arrived, followed by many other women, Arthur waved her on board where he and Marjorie stood beside the machine. 'We have a machine that can shrink things,' Arthur told the lady, whose name was Ms Hawkins.

'Really?' said Ms Hawkins, her eyes alight with hope as she took in the tiny form of Marjorie. 'Then I must insist that you shrink my buttocks! That is not a request but an order!'

Despite knowing the plan, Marjorie was still astonished. 'Umm . . . Are you sure?' she squeaked.

'I am not leaving here till you do,' she replied. 'You can use my boxtroll to put the size into,' she went on, thrusting a tiny boxtroll towards Marjorie.

'All right, if you insist . . .' Marjorie smiled. 'But I do charge!'

'I don't care. I want my buttocks reduced at any price,' Ms Hawkins insisted.

'How about ten groats a pound . . . and your boxtroll?' Marjorie said.

'Done!' Ms Hawkins snapped, and took out her purse. 'Who'd want a big boxtroll anyway, it's only the small ones that are fashionable!'

Marjorie turned to Tom and Arthur. 'Can you rig up a screen for the ladies and take the money?' They nodded. 'We need something for them to go behind and it needs a hole in it big enough for the funnel on my resizer.'

Arthur took the money while one of the pirates found a pair of scissors and cut a hole in the screen. Ms Hawkins huffed, placed the boxtroll on the deck, and then disappeared behind the screen.

'Now, I am going to put the funnel through the hole, and you must place a buttock against it. I'll extract the size, and then you'll have to place the other buttock against the funnel. When I have done that one, I'll upsize the boxtroll,' Marjorie explained, then looked up and frowned at the large resizer next to her tiny body. 'Tom, can you get one of the pirates to operate the resizer? I don't think I am big enough.'

Tom found a volunteer and Marjorie ordered him to push the funnel through the hole in the screen.

'Are you ready? Please place your first buttock against the funnel!'

'Ready!' came the cry from behind the screen.

'Extract the size!' Marjorie ordered the pirate. The pirate pulled the trigger and there was a flash and puff of smoke from behind the screen. This was followed by a delighted titter.

'Please place your second buttock against the funnel!'

'Ready!'

'Extract the size!' There was another flash and puff of smoke and yet another titter of delight.

Ms Hawkins appeared from behind the screen to gasps of admiration from the women standing at the top of the gangplank. Her figure was now as straight as a board.

With no word of thanks she marched past her fashion rivals, flaunting her non-existent buttocks, and disappeared.

Marjorie now ordered the pirate to point the other funnel at the tiny boxtroll on the deck.

'Do you understand what we are doing?' she asked the boxtroll. The boxtroll nodded and grinned.

'All right, release the size!' Marjorie ordered. There was another flash and instantly the boxtroll grew about three inches.

'Well done!' Marjorie said to the boxtroll, who was looking very pleased.

Over the course of the day many ladies were treated, including a large number who didn't have underlings as pets. This enabled Marjorie to get all the creatures back to their original size.

By late afternoon Arthur had had to find somewhere to put all the money. He now had a large barrel almost full of banknotes and coins, while on deck there were swarms of full-size underlings.

There was still a queue of ladies on the towpath, but none of them had pet underlings.

'Where are you going to put the size?' asked Arthur.

'We need to find some more shrunken underlings,' said Marjorie.

'Shall I go and get Match from the shop, and the little cabbagehead that Titus is looking after?' Tom asked.

'Yes, but what shall I do while I'm waiting? There are still loads of ladies on the towpath . . .'

'Isn't that obvious?' asked Tom.

'No,' replied Marjorie.

'Don't you want to get back to normal?' Tom asked.

'Of course. It had gone clean out of my head.'

Tom went off and returned half an hour later with everybody from the shop, to see a full-size Marjorie standing on deck, accompanied by full-size versions of Pickles and Levi.

Marjorie grinned at Willbury as he arrived.

'I am not sure I approve of this,' said Willbury.

'We didn't have much choice in the matter,' said a much less squeaky Marjorie. 'I think we would have been lynched if we had refused to co-operate. And look at all the underlings!'

Willbury looked around at all the happy big underlings and smiled. 'Well, let's

finish this off. Fish, can you bring Match here? We are going to get his size back.'

Fish came forward and placed Match on the deck in front of the screen, and Marjorie ordered the pirate to let another lady through.

Soon the remaining ladies had been treated and Match and Titus's friend regained their size.

'That's the last one!' said Marjorie triumphantly. 'Everyone's back up to full size!'

'Right!' said Willbury. 'Marjorie, could you lend me your machine for a minute?' Marjorie looked curious, but handed the machine over. Willbury placed it on the deck.

'Herbert, could you do the honours with your walloper, please?'

'But . . . ' Marjorie moved forward to get her machine.

Willbury raised a hand. 'No! We have had enough of all this resizing. Herbert will destroy the resizer and I want you to promise you are not going to try to build a new one.'

Marjorie looked rather sad. 'I suppose so . . .'

'All right then. Herbert, wallop the machine!'

There was a mighty crash and the resizer lay bent beyond recovery on the deck.

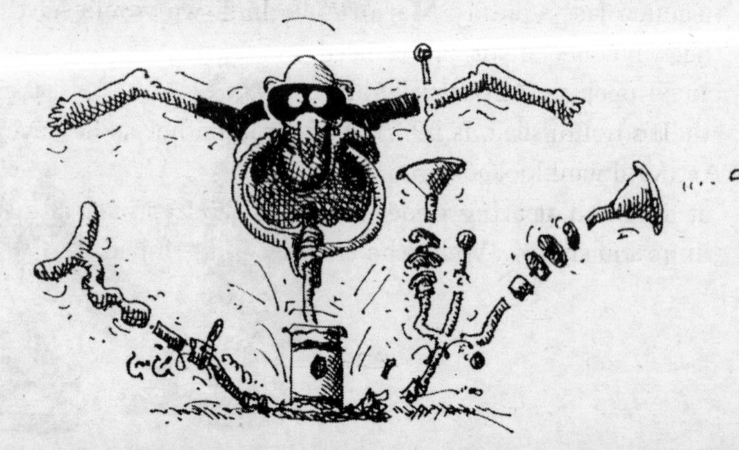

Marjorie stood staring at the ruins of her machine, while Willbury noticed the barrel full of money near Arthur.

'Don't complain, Marjorie! I think you have made rather a lot of money out of this. Perhaps you could put it to some more useful purpose than just changing the size of things.'

'And maybe something that causes less trouble,' added Grandfather.

'I did have an idea about how to distil oil and run a motor off it,' Marjorie said, looking up at the smog over the town. 'It would be a lot cleaner than steam engines.' She grinned.

'Do you think I could help?' asked Arthur.

'Of course you could. I need a bright assistant.'

That night a party was held on the laundry. The crows played harmonium, vast quantities of cocoa were drunk, and everybody danced.

'You know, for all its failings, I rather like Ratbridge,' said Willbury as they sat on the deck as the party died down.

'It's not all bad, is it?' replied Grandfather as he gave Arthur a wink.

'Not bad at all,' agreed Arthur. He looked over at all his new friends on board the laundry and grinned.

About the Author

Alan Snow is an author and illustrator, working with books, animation, film, and computers. He has written and illustrated over 160 books for children including *How Dogs Really Work* and *How Santa Really Works.* The movie, *The Boxtrolls,* is based on *Here Be Monsters!*

Worse Things Happen at Sea!

ALL ABOARD THE NAUTICAL LAUNDRY!

Arthur and his friends are about to embark on a journey to faraway shores in search of the missing secret ingredient needed for the Black Jollop miracle medicine.

It's excitement ahoy as the motley crew sets sail on the high seas of adventure!

The Boxtrolls dwell in the vast and intricate caverns under the cobblestone streets of Cheesebridge. Human legend has it the creatures are carnivorous monsters. In reality, though, they're just misunderstood oddballs who've raised an orphan human boy named Eggs.

When Eggs discovers his true identity, he finds himself in the very centre of the ongoing struggle between his Boxtroll family and cheese-loving fearmongerers. In the end, it takes a privileged little girl named Winnie to teach both Eggs and the people of Cheesebridge what it means to be human.

Novel

This activity book has everything you need to make your own Boxtrolls! Just pop out the pieces, fold at the lines, and lock in the tabs. In no time you'll have your own Eggs, Fish, Oil Can, and other curious critters!

Activity book